The Amulet of Miraculous Reversal

Or

A Grandfather's Saga

By

Tom Baldwin

Dedication This book is dedicated to Jack Vance, my favorite author. I have tried in my stumbling, bumbling way to write it in a manner you might find amusing as you look down from that great pulp mill in the sky. Jack, reading your works has taught me so much. Thank you.

Table of Contents

The Amulet of Miraculous Reversal

Or A Grandfather's Saga

The First Tale: The Poop Story

Not many summers ago the family was gathered for the Feast of Saint Clabbermilque, when gray clouds piled up in the west and a thunderstorm blew in ending my grandchildren's play in the yard and sent them scurrying into the house. Once inside, the little darlings found that the large number of adults in the various rooms ruled out running, screaming, climbing furniture and jumping off, and other such entertainments as most appeal to youngsters, so they gathered round me instead.

Grandchildren can be such a joy, and I was glad of their company. They're a man's posterity, proof that he has made his mark. This one looks like me. That one thinks like I do. She is so pretty, and reminds me of the beautiful woman I took to be my wife.

Without being told, they gathered in a half circle in front of me and a pretty blonde-haired favorite said, "Tell us a story, Grandfather,"

"Yea," came a of chorus of cries from the rest.

"What story do you want to hear," I asked.

"Tell us the poop story, grandfather, tell us the poop story," she said, eliciting another refrain of "Yeas," from the others.

Shocked, I pointed a gnarled old finger at her. "Just a minute. Where did you learn such an awful word?" I demanded. "If your mother heard you, she'd wash your mouth out with soap."

Rather than let me get the upper hand, the other darlings came to her aid. "Poop, poop, poop," they all said in a crescendo of louder and louder voices.

"Well," I said, recognizing defeat and motioning for quiet. "'Poop story' isn't a very dignified name for the account of how I came to be the richest man in all the land," I told them. "You all live in nice houses I bought for your parents, and someday my money will send each of you to the university that sits in the shadow of the king's castle. It just seems to me that an adventure that resulted in so much good for the family should have a better name than 'The Poop Story.'"

That elicited a few grumbles and exchanged glances, but I could tell they would still call it "The Poop Story."

I waited for them to settle down and when I had their attention, I began the tale they'd asked to hear. "I guess you all know that I was not always richer than even our king. Once I was a poor farmhand and traveled around this island looking for jobs so could send money home to your grandmother to feed our babies.

"So then, one summer, now long, long ago, a farmer wanted me to help harvest his field, and promised me a portion of the yield if I would work for him. Time for the reaping was fast approaching but I was still far from his farm and the only way I could get there at the agreed upon time was to take a shortcut through Goblin Woods."

I watched shivers of delicious fear pass over the grandchildren at the very mention of the forest. They trembled and yet at the same time smiled at each other. Goblin Woods is sufficiently far removed from where we live that fear of it does not keep them awake at night, but nevertheless they know it to be a horrible place, the haunt of fairies, nymphs, trolls, goblins, giants, and ghouls. That forest and its inhabitants play a big part in many frightening tales. The type you tell on a cold night, when gathered close around a flickering fire, while outside the wind moans, leafless tree branches scratch at window panes, lightning flashes reveal eerie scenes, thunder rumbles, and rain lashes the roof.

While the mention of Goblin Woods might give my grandchildren goose bumps, I remembered how, all those years ago, I had broken out in a cold sweat at just the idea of venturing into that forest.

I couldn't help but remember how just a few years before Saint Borborgast had gone into Goblin Woods to convert the trolls and had ended up the main ingredient in a stew. In the four hundred years since Christ died many had tried to bring the gospel to the forest's inhabitants. Few had ever returned from these missions and none had succeeded.

Yet it would do no good for the young ones to hear how their grandfather's knees shook as I stopped at the wood's edge to stare down that narrow trail called Theobald's Way that would lead me into it.

"I wasn't frightened," I told them. "Well, not too much, anyway. The footpath I'd chosen for my trip through the forest wasn't very wide but it looked to be well-traveled. Nothing went wrong, at least not for the first few hours. I had even started to relax a little when the trail came to a rickety looking old bridge over a deep creek bed. Just before the bridge was a pole with a sign that read, 'Toll Bridge. Ten Pence to Cross.' Below the sign hung a rusty iron pot wherein travelers might leave their payment.

"I felt my purse and knew ten pence would seriously deplete it. 'Just wade across,' I told myself and went to look over a ledge that dropped down to the creek below. Murky green water the color and consistency of pea soup greeted me. It smelled too, of rotting vegetation and stagnant water.

"'Well, how bad can it be?" I asked myself as I idly tossed a pebble into the water.

"'Bad,' I answered my own question as I watched two large swirls in the water coming from opposite directions and converging on the spot where the stone had splashed.

"'Very bad,' I revised my previous answer as the swirls came together, the water suddenly seething with furious activity, and I glimpsed a portion of something large, black and scaly as it momentarily broke the surface.

"So wading was out. I had heard of such creatures and it was said they could skeletonize a man in just minutes. A proposition I did not care to put to the test.

"I returned to the road, looked both ways, and seeing nobody in sight, decided to use the bridge without paying the toll. I was only about halfway across when the rickety bridge shook and a hideous troll climbed up over the side and confronted me. He was naked except for a dirty loincloth. His green skin hung loose in huge wattles from a body, round as it was tall. At the end of arms that hung below his knees huge hands clasped and unclasped ready to grab me and squeeze out my life.

"The troll had only one bloodshot eye, the other now reduced to just an empty socket in the middle of a scar that ran from high on his forehead and down across his cheek. I'd never seen an uglier creature and I must confess to a certain looseness of the bowels and tightening of the sphincter as I contemplated the creature.

"'I am Mangeon, and this is my bridge. I heard you come up the path,' he told me, his voice harsh and husky. 'I heard you go and look over the edge. I heard you start across my bridge. What I didn't hear was the sound of coins clinking in my iron pot.'

"'Yes,' I sputtered. 'Well, I… Well, you see, my good fellow,' I managed to stammer out. 'The pot did not seem a safe receptacle and so I intended to seek you out and pay you personally.' Reaching for my purse, I went on, 'Furthermore, since you keep such a fine strong bridge across a dangerous creek, I feel a certain gratuity is in order too.'

"'Lies,' Mangeon screeched. 'I am no mooncalf. You intended to defraud me of my rightful toll.' Then he raised a hand, index finger pointed skyward, 'I decree a penalty: a tenfold increase in payment. You must now give me one hundred pence.'

"'I do not carry such a large amount,' I said, drawing myself up. 'It is, after all, unwise in light of the footpads and vagabonds that inhabit the land. However, I can send it back to you once I arrive home,' I told him, putting a certain tone in my voice I find works well in dealing with underlings and riff raff.

"'More lies,' he shouted. 'Pay me now or you become my next meal,' and so saying, Mangeon took a step towards me.

"Backing up I asked, 'Is there nothing else I can offer?'

"'Hmm,' the troll paused in his advance to reflect for a moment. 'Possibly, 'he said. I have already dined well. You are not this day's first traveler who hoped to avoid paying my toll.' He paused and with a dirty fingernail picked at a tooth then examined the yield before going on, 'And alas, it is a lonely life I live under the bridge. I have few visitors and fewer still that arouse my ardor. So then, do you have a wife or sister that is young and comely? I know a magical spell.' His hand made a dismissive gesture, 'Well, maybe it does not rise to the level of a spell, but an enchantment at any rate. Regardless, if we both recite it together it will bring the wench here to this very spot in less than five minutes, no matter how far away she is. When she arrives, I will take the lass below and there have my way with her, impregnating her with an imp. After that both of you may go your way, and you need only return the imp to me once it is weaned.'

"Well," I paused in my tale and looking each grandchild in the eye, told them, "A man will do much to save his life, but neither the surrendering of his wife or sister to the usage of a troll nor to having her carry such a creature's spawn in her womb is among them. So even if it was to cost me my life, I lied to the foul creature, telling it, 'I am not married and my only sister died of the bloody flux this past year.'

"'Too bad,' Mangeon said, sounding truly disappointed. Then seeming to brighten up he added, 'At least I will not go hungry.'

“Backing away once more, I said, ‘Wait, I have something you might like.’ So saying I reached into my pouch and brought out some honeycomb wrapped in brown paper. ‘Let me pass, and I will give you this honeycomb in place of the toll. I ate some yesterday, it is very sweet and easily worth more than ten pence.’

“His single eye seemed to come alive with avarice. I’d heard that trolls have a weakness for sweets. He reached out for the honeycomb but I backed away once more. ‘Are we agreed, you will let me cross in return for the honey?’

“‘No,’ was his answer. ‘But I will take the honey and it shall be my dessert after devouring you.’

“Getting desperate, and thinking that if I could just once get by Mangeon, I was sure I could outrun him, I said, ‘Here,’ and tossed the honeycomb high into the air so that it would fall behind him. I was hoping he would back up to catch it and thereby give me space to get by. He did back up, indeed the troll backed up too much, so that he suddenly found himself teetering on the edge of the bridge.

“His arms windmilled as he sought to regain his balance. Seeing my opportunity, I stepped forward, said, ‘Eat me, would you?’ Then I placed the tip of my walking staff in the center of his chest and shoved. With a cry of startled rage Mangeon went over backwards and fell with a huge splash in the middle of the creek. As I watched, swirls such as I had seen earlier, a dozen of them, at least, from up and down the creek, converged on the spot where he had gone in. The troll barely had time to rise to the surface before the first swirl arrived. Beating the water with his fists he bellowed out his rage at me, and the sad turn his life had suddenly taken. As more and more swirls arrived, his yells and beating at the water increased in frenzy. Twice he rose with one of the scaly black creatures in his hands. These he tossed up on the creek's bank where they writhed in the thick grass. Finally, their numbers grew until there were too many for him and he was pulled under.

"For a few moments I watched the water's surface roil with the frantic battle that was taking place below, then decided I should be on my way. *If Mangeon manages to somehow survive,* I thought to myself, *I fear he will fail to see the positive side of this experience. Nor will he be persuaded to kinder and gentler treatment of strangers like me. In fact, what little I've seen of him suggests that if he emerges from the water, he will instead be in a vile and wicked temper. Best I be nowhere around, for however unjustly, that wrath will, most likely, focus on me.*

"After leaving the bridge, I ran for the first mile and then slowed to a fast walk for the next. Breath coming in gasps, I finally stopped, hid in some bushes off the trail, and watched the way I'd come. I waited there a good quarter hour and nothing followed, so I relaxed and moved on.

"As the day approached its end, I had yet to find an inn in which to spend the night. Then to make matters worse a storm that had been brewing on the horizon bore down on me, and so with the approach of darkness came a cool wind and some heavy drops of rain. I knew only a fool would bed down on the forest floor where ghosts and ghouls were known to wander after dark. But what was I to do? Climb a tree and spend the night up there clinging to a branch in the wind and rain? I was afraid I was going to have no choice, when coming around a bend in the trail, there ahead of me in the deepening twilight I saw something large and dark, rising higher than the trees.

"It proved to be the ruins of an ancient castle. As darkness gathered, I climbed over stones, bricks, and broken beams looking for some area that had retained enough roof to shelter me from the cold wet night that was falling fast. Finally, I found a dry corner where I could sit as the last glimmer of day receded.

"I gathered dry wind -blown leaves from the other corners and piled them so I would have a place to rest. They did prove soft enough, but there was a musky smell to them that I didn't like.

"I soon found out where the odor came from. I was not alone in the castle. Rats by the scores scurried about everywhere. They were the source of the smell. To make matters worse, something else, something huge moved about in the wreckage too. I felt rather than saw this presence, a darker darkness amidst the black of the night. I couldn't help but wonder who or what it was. I was ready to flee, but thankfully it paid me no mind. It was busy about other pursuits and every once in a while I would hear sudden movement followed by hysterical squeaking from one of the rats, squeaking that was quickly silenced by the crunching of small bones.

"Too frightened to sleep I huddled there. Finally the storm ended and the moon shone between the clouds. It was well past midnight when the ghost of Mangeon found me. I could see him coming as he floated over the rubble. He glowed with a pale greenish light that showed him savaged and torn by the creek's scaly black inhabitants. Great hunks of flesh had been ripped from his frame, as was most of his scalp. He was also missing his left foot, and an arm. 'I have come for you,' he announced. 'You will return with me to the bridge, there you will also enter the waters beneath it.' I was too frightened to move as his one arm with its huge hand reached for me, but at that instant the creature that hunted the darkness for rats came between us.

"'Leave,' I heard it tell Mangeon. 'This traveler may be of use to me.'

"'But Master, this one owes me his life,' said Mangeon.

"'You think I care about your petty debts? Leave.'

"'As you wish then, sir,' Mangeon said, as if the ghost of the troll would not even think of arguing with that black emptiness that had come between us. 'But first I wish to at least lay a mordant on. I curse him with…'

"'Be gone,' the darkness interrupted, and Mangeon was gone. The ghost just vanished. One second I could see him glowing there in the dark, the next moment he disappeared like a candle flame blown out.

"'Thank you,' I tried to tell the darkness but it was gone too, and so I found myself spending the next few hours worrying over how I might be of use to the dark creature and also the troll's incomplete curse. Was it operative if only partially delivered? I hoped not.

"Finally dawn came. I looked around to find I had spent the night in what had at one time been some sort of alchemist's or sorcerer's workroom. Old books by the dozen lay amongst shattered shelves. The volumes were in tatters, gnawed and torn apart by the rats, for it seemed they found the leather bindings nutritious and that the pages made excellent nesting material.

“All about I saw strange tools and apparatus that lay broken on the floor or under tumbled-down walls. From beneath one great stone a skeleton’s leg appeared. Walking around the stone I found the body of what must have been the castle’s former owner crushed where a heap of rocks and bricks had fallen on him. The bones were clothed in fine, if now rotted, cloth embroidered with strange signs and runes. Startled, I was backing away from the body when I saw a bracelet on one bony wrist. A red stone glowed at its center and strange markings adorned its surface.

“Frightened as I was, I could not leave such a treasure behind. The dead man no longer had need of it. So I leaned quickly to collect it. As I removed the bracelet from the body the ruins began to tremble and more stones crashed down from the few remaining walls; then the very ground under the castle shook and earth itself let out a loud groaning sigh. What had I done? Was it a groan of pain and rage, or relief? Who was to know? Holding the bracelet tightly I fled the castle.

“Again, I ran for about a mile before I felt safe enough to slow to a walk. Only then did I pause to look over my new treasure. It was made of an iron gray metal that felt warm to the touch. The red stone looked to be a pigeon blood ruby. Covering the bracelet were strange decorations and runes that I could not read. ‘An amulet,’ I told myself as I put it on my wrist.

* * *

“Noon approached and I'd not eaten in over a day so I was

thrilled when I found an apple tree growing beside the way. The apples, while full sized, were still mostly green and not yet ripe, but I was very hungry. Thinking of Mangeon the troll and the sigh from beneath the castle, I was a little frightened at the idea of what might happen should I just help myself.

"'If someone within hearing claims these apples for their own, let them speak,' I shouted. I waited but heard no answer. 'If someone within hearing owns these apples and allows hungry wayfarers eat freely of them, they are indeed a blessed and altruistic person. May the gods smile on them,' I raised my voice again. I waited once more but still no one spoke.

"Satisfied I'd taken adequate precautions, I helped myself to a half dozen of the largest apples and munching them, hurried on my way, hoping I could be out of the forest by dark. When the apples were gone I felt much better, but only temporarily. Soon my stomach began to rumble and I started to pass great quantities of gas. Then an hour or so later an ache that got progressively worse filled my lower digestive tract, and I suddenly felt a great need to answer the call of nature.

"At that time Theobald's Way lead along the edge of a large meadow. Of late I had occasionally encountered other people on the trail and being of a modest nature, I did not want to just crouch down to do my business where someone might happen upon me. Looking around I saw a good-sized bush about fifty feet off the path and near the meadow's center. Thinking it would give me the cover my modesty demanded, I hurried towards it across the intervening grass.

"Halfway there I felt a sudden and violent cramp twist my insides and I knew the time had come. I hoped nobody was watching for I could do nothing but drop my pants and squat there on the meadow, letting my bowel void itself in a great flux.

“'Poop, poop, poop,' my grandchildren interrupted the story.

“‘Yes, yes’ I told them. ‘The Poop Story, so settle down and listen carefully.’”

They gave me another round of “poops,” just to show who was really in charge, but then grew quiet and attentive again.

“‘You see, children,’ I told them, ‘I was just enjoying that sense of relief that comes with a good… Well, let’s just say I was feeling better, when I heard cries of outrage and indignity. ‘What?’ I asked myself. Then the air around me seemed to shimmer, and before my eyes the meadow changed into a beautiful park. What had seemed to be a small patch of grassy ground now appeared to be a huge field encompassing a hundred or more acres. The bush that I’d hurried towards swelled and changed into a lovely castle with ramparts rising tier upon tier, while all around me I saw a crowd of fairies. The humble meadow with a single bush at its center was not what it had seemed, but was a fairy kingdom instead.

“The fairies were all dressed in their finest clothes as if for a party and spread out on the grass to every side of me were tablecloths covered with what was truly the most wonderful feast I had ever seen. Meats, fruits, vegetables, and sweets were piled high on great golden platters, and it was in the very heart of this assemblage of fine foods that I squatted.

“One fairy, wearing a crown, approached me. ‘I am King

Thrombay and you, sir, are a cad and a scoundrel. It is Fripsen See that you have befouled and our Harvest Feast you have wrecked.'

"'I am truly sorry,' I told him. 'I didn't do so on purpose. I didn't see you. I didn't know you were here or what you were about. You have my deepest apologies.'

"'They are not enough. You exposed yourself before these, the most delicate of ladies, the finest flowers of fairy nobility. Then you befouled our food and filled the air with a horrible smell that will linger in our park for a long time. No, I tell you, just an apology will not do.'

"'Very well then, I had thought to join your feast, but I will leave instead,' I said in a haughty manner, and then turned to go. However the Fairy King said if I tried to leave he would put a curse on me and my family

"'Leave? Not yet you won't," he said. 'Your deeds cry out for fairy justice.'

"I had heard of fairy justice and wanted none of it, but what was I to do?

"The fairy king turned to his people. 'What shall we do with him?' he asked them.

"'Turn him into a toad,' came a cry from the rear.

"'Fill him with worms and let them eat their way out,' a lady spoke

"'No, no," said the king. 'Fairy law decrees that punishment should fit the crime. I see no correlation between his foul deed and toads or worms.'

"'Turn him into a spider,' came that first voice from the rear again.

"'No,' said the king. 'Transformation could be a just punishment, but what we change him into must relate to his crime.'

"'Draw his nose out to a length of three feet and give him the olfactory sensitivity of a hound that he might always smell every evil stench that wafts across the land,' said a gentlemen.

"'Hum,' said the king and putting hand to chin seemed to think about this one.

"'Turn him into a cockroach,' came the voice from the rear again.

"With a shake of his head, the king said, 'How many times must I tell you, correlation, correlation.'

"'Mayhap you might curse him with a vile stench to his body that will not wash off, nor can be covered by perfumes,' came another's suggestion. 'Let him be a pariah to his own as he will always be to us.'

"'Maybe,' said the king and seemed to ponder that suggestion too.

"'Turn him into a dung beetle,' the squeaky voice from the rear tried again.

"That brought the kings head up with a jerk. 'Perfect,' said Thrombay, 'Perfect. I will transform him into a dung beetle. That will be fairy justice at its very finest.'

"'But this is unfair,' I protested. 'For a crime to have been committed I must have had malice in my heart, I must have desired to wreck your picnic. I am just an innocent man with a bad case of indigestion caused by eating under ripened apples and who consequently had to relieve himself in a hurry or soil his clothes.'

"'Nevertheless, you ruined our meal,' said King Thrombay.

'Surely you can see that something must be done to right the scales. Such an affront cannot go unanswered. A penalty must be exacted.' He seemed to stand a little taller and sound even more pompous as he continued, 'So then now, stand ready to receive the transforming ray.'

"The other fairies gathered in a semicircle behind their king to watch. With a great flourish he drew forth a wand. Then saying some sort of incantation I could not understand, King Thrombay drew three great circles over his head with the wand and then dropped it to point at me.

"'Wait,' I begged as I covered my face with my hands. But it was not to be, and the transforming ray lanced out from the wand and straight at my head. It did not hit me, however, instead it was drawn in by the amulet I wore on my wrist. There was a great flash of light as the two magics struggled. But the contest was not equal, and ended quickly. The ruby flashed with a brilliant light and the fairies' magic was bounced back at them in a wide fan of luminescence that struck all of them. The air suddenly filled with cries of surprise, followed by outrage, and finally horror and woe as they realized their fate.

"As I watched, one after another they all shrank away to become dung beetles. I heard one particular squeaky voice, the one that had suggested my fate, now full of consternation cry "No! No! Not me! Not me!" The voice sounding tinier and tinnier with each syllable as its owner changed from fairy to insect. When the process was complete, I quickly backed away in disgust as I saw them all now struggling across the grass, hurrying to be the first to arrive at the deposit I had left on their meadow.

"I looked at the amulet I wore in wonder. It felt a little warmer than before, but no marks could be seen on its surface and the ruby glowed with the same red light. Instinctually I gave it a kiss of gratitude and then looked around. My first thought was to get back on the road and out of the forest as fast as possible. I was just about to do so when I had a second thought: Fairy gold!

"Quickly I turned towards their castle, which seemed to waver in my sight. Without the fairies to give it substance it was reverting to a bush. I knew I must hurry if I planned to enter, but by the time I reached it, the castle had become transparent. As I stood there wondering what to do, it faded completely away, becoming just a bush once more. Muttering a curse I started to walk from the meadow when I saw sunlight glint off something within former castle Thickly crowded branches made it hard to see, but there within was the fairies' pot of gold. The wealth it contained was real, not fairy stuff, and had survived the end of their world.

"I stuffed my purse, pouch, pack and pockets with enough gold and jewels to make me a very rich man. Once more I started to leave the meadow. As I passed the spot in the field where I had relieved myself I noticed that one of the dung beetles gathered there wore a miniature gold crown. As I leaned over to inspect him, Thrombay spoke to me in a small voice, 'I see it now. You are no doubt the fellow who released the spirit of the thrice cursed magician Rhialto the Forlorn from his imprisonment below his fallen down castle.'

"'Did he live off eating live rats?' I asked.

"'Yes, such an unsavory dietary limitation was indeed one of his curses,' the dung beetle king allowed.

"'Well,' I told Thrombay thinking better of being too forth

coming, 'I know nothing of this Rhialto, but just this morning I came into possession of a wondrous amulet that turned your evil intentions against my person back on you and your fellow fairies.'

"'Yes,' he said. 'Just after breakfast news of Rhialto's release swept through the forest, which could only mean someone else now possessed The Amulet of Miraculous Reversal. I should have checked before attempting your alteration.'

"'Alteration you call it now? And that is your only regret? Just that you did not check before cursing me?' I asked, my anger growing. I thought seriously of stepping on the vile insect and he seemed to realize his mistake, because he changed the subject.

"'So, I see you've helped yourself to our wealth,' he said, pointing a brown chitinous leg towards my pack that brimmed with gold.

"'Well, I felt you would have no further need of it,' I offered in excuse.

"'True, true,' said the king sounding as if he accepted my reasons for taking the gold. 'It seems so long ago, but only this morning I found myself marveling at how the sunlight glinted off my gold and refracted through my jewels. Yet now, just a few hours later, I find those same baubles dull and unappealing. Now I have a new standard of beauty!'" Said the insect king.

"Turning he gestured, 'Notice this dung ball I have constructed.' He waved his antennas towards it with pleasure. 'A sphere of both geometric and utilitarian perfection. I will roll it around the meadow with pride. Are you not in awe of it?'

"'Well.... So then you hold no hard feelings toward me?' I

changed the subject.

"'None.'

"'That being the case, I forgive you too,' I said feeling magnanimous. 'It is not good to carry about resentments and grudges. Better to be at peace with one's fellow creatures.'

"The beetle nodded in agreement. 'I had been a fairy king for a thousand years. It had begun to grow dull. You have opened new vistas on the world for me.'

"'Then might I ask a small favor of you? Last night a troll named Mangeon attempted to put me under a bane. Could you bless me? Make something good happen for me, to counteract his curse.'

"'Mangeon! Mangeon who kept a toll bridge?'

"'Yes, the same.'

"'You must be mistaken. Yesterday Mangeon slipped from his bridge and into Hell Creek where he was set upon by the Tanatoid Eels. I fear he is no longer numbered among the living. It couldn't have been him that tried to curse you.'"

"'Two items,' I told Thrombay. 'First Mangeon did not slip and fall from his bridge. In fact, he was pushed. I know this to be true because it was I who gave him the fatal thrust that toppled him into the creek. He was intent upon eating me, and being unready to die, I took measures to preserve my life. That those measures led to his demise… Well, he should have known better than to threatened to eat me.'"

"'Quite right, quite right, and I must say there, son, you have been quite busy since entering our forest. Mangeon does not eat fairies. Their meat is bitter to his taste. However, long has he prowled the forest trails, hiding in bushes with a rope lasso to snare fairy maidens which he then deflowers. That he is gone is good news, and that he went at the hand of another even better,' said the dung beetle king.

"'Well, the second thing I wanted to tell you is that it *was* indeed Mangeon's ghost that wished to curse me. Even being devoured and experiencing the alimentary canals of various Tanatoid Eels has not mellowed him. His spirit remains cruel and vindictive, full of both anger and rage, and however unjustly, it is at me that he has directed that wrath. It was my hope you might be able to turn aside this fury, or at least counter balance his bane with a boon of your own.'

"'Certainly,' said Thrombay. 'I will try.' He paused a moment to consider then continued, 'May your bowel always be regular, may your movements never be too loose or too hard."

"'Well, yes,' I told the dung beetle king, sounding a little bitter. 'I apologize if I sound a bit disappointed, I'd hoped you might bless me with a long and happy life, or some such boon.'

"Thrombay paused to wipe his feelers with his front legs before saying, 'I thought you'd be most pleased with the blessing. I suppose it must be the new focus of my existence that colors my judgment and leaves me thinking a healthy lower intestine a thing to be desired above all.' Again he paused, this time to work on a small flaw he found on his dung ball. As he sought to repair it, he went on, 'A problem herein arises. Dung beetle blessings, while not limited in scope, are limited to a total of three things. I have already given you two: regularity and proper stool consistency. I am limited to one more item, yet you ask for two, both a long and happy life.'

"'If I had to settle for one…' I started to say, but was interrupted by Thrombay.

"'Nevertheless,' he continued, 'I think I see a way to give you each of them with one blessing.' So saying, he straightened his crown and then lifted a long brown foreleg in benediction. 'And lastly, I bless you with wonderful grandchildren.'

"Again I was not entirely satisfied with my blessing. However, since Thrombay had gone back to work on his dung ball, was no longer paying me any mind, and I wanted to be out of Goblin Woods by nightfall, I thanked him and hurried on down Theobald's Way.

"It is only in recent years that I have come to see that that last blessing as the best I could have asked for, that everything I wanted in life was summed up in it. Wonderful grandchildren. For what more could a man desire?"

And so saying, I gathered them into my arms.

The Amulet of Miraculous Reversal

Or A Grandfather's Saga

The Second Tale: The Future Mage

Just ten paces from the field into the forest. Just ten paces from bright sunlight to deep shadows under huge old oaks. Yet that ten paces set my heart to racing like it hadn't since I'd been in Rome when the Visigoths sacked it twenty years ago.

I was lucky then. I got away with my life and not much else but being alive at the end of that day had felt so good. Me and some others had commandeered a boat and fled down the Tiber River. I remember how good it felt to leave Rome behind us and see the Mediterranean spreading in front of us.

Would I be so lucky this time too, and live to tell the story of this trip into the Goblin Woods? I had good reason to worry, because the forest is home to ogres and giants, sirens and fairies, witches and wizards, dragons and trolls. Creatures that in other lands and places are the stuff of nightmares yet are all too real to us who live on the island of Tredagar.

You mustn't get the wrong idea, however. Our island is really a good place to live, so long as you stay out of the Goblin Woods. Here we are safe from most of what is happening on the mainland. The Atlantic protects us. Boats are scarce and the formidable league upon league of open water has kept us safe from those wild men of the north who are raping and pillaging their way across Europe.

Even knowing the mayhem is far distant, I lay awake some nights, haunted by memories of barbarians howling through the streets of Rome, streets acrid with the smoke of burning books and alight with fires that heralded both the end of civilization, and the coming of the long night.

But, I am getting ahead of myself. You must be wondering why, if the Goblin Woods are so bad, that I would enter them under any circumstances? Vanity, I guess. A desire to please. To live up to expectations. All three, probably.

The chain of events that resulted in my entering the woods started about two weeks ago, when I was approached by my grandson Angwyn. He is a tall thin boy, ruddy of complexion, with a personality old beyond his years. "Grandfather," he told me. "I have decided I want to become a great magician, just like you."

"Well," I said. "Well…ah…" my voice trailing off as I stalled for time. The problem is I am not a magician, I am not a mage, and I am not a diabolist. I am none of those things, not by any stretch of the imagination. I know very little of the thaumaturgical arts. However, I am not surprised that people mistakenly think I am a wizard of some sort. After all, I do have a very powerful magical appurtenance that I wear at all times: The Amulet of Miraculous Reversal.

So there I am hemming and hawing while my grandson looks on, a questioning expression on his face. Isn't it strange how children, especially those in their teens, seem to know their parents are human and have all the flaws that come with that status, but see their grandparents as some sort of lofty beings, existing above mankind's foibles? I have to admit I find it an agreeable situation to be in. The adulation of those you care most about can be most gratifying, except at times like this, when you are forced to reveal yourself as something less than the demigod they think you to be. I didn't want to let Angwyn down, but what was I to do?

I think he must have seen the consternation on my face. "Oh, I will understand if you don't wish to help me," he said and I could hear the disappointment in his voice. Then he stood a little straighter. "But you must know that I am strong, I am brave, and I like to think I am intelligent. Are these not the qualities you expect in a magician?"

Add compassion to that list and it would be a fine foundation on which to build a career in magic. However, my experience with magicians has not revealed many with such characteristics. Rather I have found them a pompous, self-centered lot, greedy and highly competitive. Each striving to out-do and overpower all others.

I looked at Angwyn and remembered that many years before I had been given a blessing by a king. In it he promised me "wonderful grandchildren." When they started coming along, I in turn promised myself that given wonderful grandchildren, I would do all I could see that they received chances and opportunities to achieve their dreams and get ahead on whatever life path they chose for themselves.

So it was that my mind raced, searching for a solution. One that might allow me to both help my grandson and retain that level of regard I so enjoyed. And I hit on it. Spinning to face Angwyn I put a hand on each of his shoulders and said, “Spring Equinox. It’s coming.”

“So,” he looked puzzeled.”

“It’s more than just a festive time of dances and feasts, with our homes and villages festooned in flower garlands. It is also the time of the annual Magicians’ Fair in the heart of The Goblin Woods.”

Angwyn shook his head, a questioning look on his face.

“Normally,” I told him, “You know that I anyone who cares about their health and well-being avoids those woods, and enters only if they have to. Once a year, however, at the time of the fair, by some agreement, a moratorium of sorts exists that allows any and all who wish to visit the fair to do so unmolested by the wood’s inhabitants.

This could be my way of retaining my grandson’s esteem. I put an arm around his shoulder and pulled him against myself. “Angwyn, I am afraid you labor under a false impression. I am no magician. I have this,” I pulled back my sleeve and held up my wrist so he could see my amulet, a gray circlet of metal covered in runes and set with a red ruby-like stone that glowed with an inner fire. “It protects me from all magic sent against me and turns it back on those who would harm me. But I don’t command it. I just wear it and am protected by it.”

I could see the look of disappointment on his face. So I hurried on, “However, if you really desire the life of a magician I think I know a way you might become one. In just a few days it will be Equinox and time for the magicians’ fair. It is in the heart of the haunted forest. There they flock from all over to the woods to buy and trade.

Forgive me if I am telling you stuff you already know, but others can attend it too. You must speak to your parents of this. If they give their permission, you and I should be able to go there and, maybe find a wizard that will take you on as an apprentice. Barring that we can attempt to buy books and items of magical import that would allow you to study and work on your own to become a magician. What do you say?" He didn't have to answer. I could see his reply in his happy smile.

I muttered on a while longer, trying to sound reassuring, but in my heart I wondered if I would be able to pull this off. A directive is a directive, a rule a rule, but can you really trust fairies with their tricks or ogres with their hunger for human flesh to obey? We were going to find out.

* * *

It was not too long until the day arrived for our trip to the Magician's Fair and heart pounding, I made those ten steps into the Goblin Woods, and then another ten, and so on…

I must admit the morning was beautiful. After a while my fears subsided. White clouds chased each other across a blue sky. For miles our path through Goblin Woods ran alongside a brook that gurgled over rocks or spread into quiet pools. Tall oaks grew to either side and shaded the road with a dappled sunlight. The trees were home to countless birds and squirrels that chirped or scolded as we passed. It seemed so peaceful that one might almost forget that at any other time but Equinox, danger would lurk everywhere.

Angwyn was fascinated by the woods. He stopped to pick flowers and mushrooms, showing them to me. "I have been studying. I think this one is used in a potion that allows you to walk through other people's dreams," or "Such beauty can only engender more beauty. I must learn how this flower's essence can be used to make beautiful maidens even more comely." Another flower was held out for me to smell its heady aroma. "I'm going to copy this scent."

Idealistic? Overly so? Such would seem to be the case. However I began to see that if he ever became the magician he longed to be, he would, unlike most others in that trade, put any powers he gained to good use. My grandfather's heart puffed with pride and it made me more and more determined that our mission should succeed.

* * *

Tredagar is made of soft crumbly rock. I was reminded of that by the number landslides we had to make our way around. Large boulders blocked the road and/or dammed the creek. Each year the ocean washes away huge amounts of our island too. At the rate it is disappearing into the sea, I suspect a thousand years from now will see Tredagar gone, reduced to a few rocks jutting from the ocean's swell, their tops white with bird droppings and their base's a place for basking seals. Will men remember Tredagar then, or will she be a place of legend like Lyonesse or Atlantis? Who's to know.

While being forgotten may or may not be Tredagar's fate, it surely will be mine. A few generations will see me lost in obscurity. I'll be forgotten, only a weathered lichen encrusted rock in a weedy churchyard to tell people I once existed. A rock that may elicit a question or two by children visiting our family plot, and pointing and asking, "Who was he?" But I'll not even know the question was asked. Six feet of sod and dirt will muffle the sound of their voices and pad of their feet. I'll be unaware they were even there.

My one chance to leave a mark on history is through my family, my grandchildren and their grandchildren and on down the generations. So I spend my time and means on the ones I can, endeavoring to set them on the right path and hope for the best. Angwyn…? *Well*, I determined, as I stepped around another rock pile, *Damn if he isn't going to be one of those successes I seek.*

* * *

We'd left my home shortly after sunrise, and leading our pack mule, arrived at the site of the fair about two in the afternoon. There Theobald's Way, which was our route through the woods, opened out onto a large meadow. One moment we were surrounded by great old oaks, their twisted mossy branches allowing just a hint of sky and sunlight. Then the road opened on a huge expanse of about five acres. The giant trees grew right up to its edge. The transition to grass was abrupt, no stumps, no fallen snags. The grassy meadow looked new mown except for patches of flowers here and there. Mostly yellow, but some lavender, and others red, the blossoms giving the meadow an inviting look. At first glance, the impression was one of natural perfection, but as I thought on things, I realized that magic had most likely been at work. Some wizard had cast a spell over what is most likely a weedy pasture full of mangy goats. If you'd come by a week ago or came a week from now, you would be twisting and turning, hoping to avoid stepping in things you'd rather not, going around patches of thistle, or dodging a Billy goat bent on butting you . Still, I had to admire whoever was responsible for their excellent taste. They had created a charming place to hold a fair.

"Here we are," I told Angwyn with a sweep of my arm.

Around the edge of the meadow, booths rose while others stood complete. Soon a person would be able to buy, sell, or trade for almost anything having to do with the thaumaturgical arts. I put an arm around my grandson's shoulder and reminded him, "I am really hoping we will find a magician that will take you on as apprentice, or failing that we can purchase objects with which you can study the magical arts for yourself."

On the north side of the meadow stood the Inn of Laughing Moon and Crying Sun, an ancient-looking edifice of three stories with many gables and chimneys. It was constructed mostly of roughly hewn gray stone. Its large double-doored entrance was thrown open in welcome.

As we crossed the threshold we were greeted by the innkeeper, one Fynbar, a grizzled old faun. His goat ears, legs and tail were all showing their years, the tip of his left horn was broken off and the fur on his legs missing in large patches.

A lifetime of experience has taught me that innkeepers are cut from the same cloth as lawyers and politicians, and thus an avaricious lot, over charging guests while under serving them. When dealing with such, I find it wisest to act as if I am a rich (which I am), pompous (on occasion) and self-indulgent man (of this I am innocent) and used to getting my own way (don't we all wish for this?). So early on I let them know I have high expectations.

The above being the case, even before Fynbar could utter a word,

I tossed a purse heavy with coin on his table. It landed with a satisfying chink. "My grandson and I will require separate, but adjoining private rooms," I told him. "I want them far from the taproom and its sounds of drunken revelry which I expect will go on all night. They must not be too close to the latrine ditch either. I cannot abide the noises and smells accompanying the activities going on there either. I think rooms on the third floor near the front might meet our needs," I paused a moment as if in thought before going on. When the innkeeper appeared about to speak I jumped in again, "I expect, of course, that the mattress ticking of our beds has been smoked recently to kill any vermin present and then stuffed with fresh hay. I have no desire to share my sleeping accommodations with fleas, lice, or bedbugs. If you have not fumigated, you must see to it immediately. Now as to our meals. We will expect the very best of what the inn has to offer, dished out in generous portions. Oh, and no drunken serving girls to wait on us. Angwyn, my grandson, is of a delicate nature and is especially disturbed by uncouth behavior in females. We will want the girl who serves us to be clean, neither fat in the haunch nor bony of limb. If she were buxom that would not be amiss, but I do not require it. However, and on this I insist, she that she be clean, smelling of neither fish nor the barnyard."

Only having said all that did I let the innkeeper speak. Much to my disappointment he said, "In normal circumstances I could accede to your requests. But the Magician's fair begins tomorrow and the demands on my inn are far in excess of its capacity. There are no private rooms for the next few days. The smallest rooms will hold four guests, the larger ones more. If I put you in one of the small rooms I can, however, arrange for you two to share a mattress. The room's other mattress will go to another two men you will likely not know. As luck would have it, I do have such a room on the third floor and in the front as you requested."

"This is intolerable," I said while slapping the tabletop. "As I already said, Angwyn is of a fragile disposition. What if these other fellows you propose to room with us are coarse in nature, having body odor and given to snoring and passing noxious smelling gases in their sleep?"

"Well, I could give the two of you exclusive use of the hayloft in the barn. You would be alone there. But the animals below make a good deal of noise in the night and the roosters rise early. Furthermore, it is located hard on the latrine ditch which you wished to avoid."

I could see further bluster would not get me what I wanted, so I told him, "I am not happy. However, we will take the third floor room, provided the cost is reduced from your normal charge by a significant amount due to the inconveniences we must suffer."

"I might reduce my fees by a slight amount," Fynbar allowed. Then pointing a long boney index finger towards the ceiling, he stated, "But the overarching and guiding principles must be the Law of Supply and Demand and the old capitalist maxim, 'Whatever the traffic will bear.' There are few rooms in my inn and many people clambering after them. Their very scarcity argues for a premium price, not a reduction. However, in light of your grandson's fragile condition I will lower my fee by one groat."

"What? Surely you jest," I said shaking my head. And so began the bickering which took a number of minutes and involved some raised voices on both of our parts before agreement was reached.

When coins finally exchanged hands Fynbar said, “Good, now I think we can make up for some of your disappointment when we serve you dinner. This evening’s fare is a specialty of the house: roast duckling stuffed with mushrooms, leeks, and onions. It is served with bread loaves still warm from the oven and large beakers of my finest mead.” He paused and sniffed the air, “Take a deep breath and you can smell the aroma of the roasting fowl now. Oh, and I have a toothsome young serving wench I will assign to your table. You should find her even more pleasing than the food.”

“Well then,” I said. “I am dusty and sweaty from the road. Are you too busy to provide me with a warm bath? I want to freshen up. Then Angwyn and I wish to go out and see some of the booths that are already open.”

“By all means. I am happy meet this request. There will, of course, be a surcharge.”

“Of course there will be,” I said trying to keep frustration from voice.

“Let me show you where you will be staying,” he said and motioned to one of his workers to get our trunk. The room was not well appointed. The walls were yellow and bare. Two mattresses lay on the wooden floor. They took up most of the space and comprised the only furniture to be found. One was worn and badly stained while the other looked rather new. I knew instantly which one Angwyn and I would sleep on. A single window let in light and air. Near the door a candleholder hung on the wall. At least it was equipped with a large candle that should give us some light all night long.

Seeing the frown on my face Fynbar gave me no time to complain before telling us, “I must leave you now as other guests need my attention. But just give my people ten minutes to heat some water and drag the copper tub up here to your room and your bath will be ready.”

* * *

I put on fresh clothes after an extended ablution. It is remarkable how a bath and clean cloth next to one’s skin can refresh a body. I was about to remark on just this fact to Angwyn when there was a knock and the innkeeper showed two men into our room. He introduced them as Turi and Nosdab and told us that they would be sharing the room.

Turi looked to be a typical merchant. He wore clean tasteful clothes, and his full head of blonde hair was as neatly trimmed as his mustache. He pulled a large wooden trunk into the room behind himself.

Nosdab, however, was something to behold. He was an older man who wore a black woolen gown that hung to the floor and covered his arms all the way to his wrists. On his head he had a conical cap the upper tip of which rose a good two feet higher than the top of his head. Rather than remove it, he ducked when entering the room. The hat too was black and covered with what looked like constellations of stars, but I recognized none of them as being from our earthly skies. Nosdab wore his gray hair and beard long and in tight curls that seemed unkempt to me. He also had a strange odor about himself. It wasn’t an unpleasant aroma, just unusual one, like nothing I had ever smelled before. Nosdab too dragged a large trunk into the room.

Angwyn and I smiled as we were introduced, then we politely took our leave so we could go view some of the early booths out on the meadow. As we made for the door Turi asked Fynbar if he could use the bath that still sat in the middle of the room.

"Of course." Fynbar said then stuck a finger into the water before going on, "The water has gone tepid, but has only been used once and while I would not drink it, it still seems fairly clean. Fresh enough for bathing purposes. So the charge will be just two groats."

"Just so," said Turi. "It is tepid and has been used already. I think a fairer price would be a single groat."

How the bargaining went I don't know. By then we were down the hall with the door closed behind us. However, innkeepers, as I already pointed out, are a grasping, avaricious lot used to driving hard bargains. My guess, Turi and his money were soon parted.

* * *

A few minutes later found us out on the meadow. People were busy setting up their spots. Most were setting out wares but not ready to sell and resented "Early Birds" like Angwyn and I nosing about and asking questions as they worked. I made mental black marks against a few I found exceptionally surly and vowed not return even after they opened. Some, however, had finished setting up and were ready to start selling. As I looked for one of these I suddenly heard a great pounding. As intended, it got my attention, and seemed portentous so I grabbed

Angwyn's arm and led him towards the sound. It came from a purple tent, out in front of which a boy stood beating on a drum.

When a large crowd had gathered a small wispy-haired man in yellow coat and green pants came out of the tent and joined the boy on the stage set in front of it. With the man's arrival the boy ceased his pounding and exited the platform. Now having everyone's attention to himself the small man held up a piece wood about a foot square with strange runes carved on one side and thick gray metal covering the other.

In a high, squeaky voice he announced, "Friends and fellow spellbinders, necromancers, divinators, seers, sages, and what like, I am Hezekiah, a poor man reduced to tomb robbing by my poverty. I have a wondrous tale to tell you. I hold before you a piece of the coffin of the famous sorceress Messala, acknowledged as one of the ten most powerful wizards of all time. She has been dead lo these two hundred fifty years, yet even to this day she has many followers. If they knew what I had done, they would look unkindly upon my depredations. For you see, it was at great risk to myself that I broke into her crypt and brought away her coffin. A risk I took that I might share the bounty of her grave goods with you, my fellow magicians.

"When I opened her casket I found that it had a curious construction, in that it was lined with lead that sealed it up airtight. This had the effect of keeping almost any of the substance of Messala from escaping into the surrounding ambiance where it would dissipate. However, over the intervening centuries a tiny amount of her vitality did transude into the lead and eventually into the surrounding wood too."

"Now as each of you must be aware, Messala was rich and lived in a large manse east of here near Cross Hollows. While alive she attracted money like iron to a lodestone. And just so, these sections of her coffin, permeated with her very essence, will draw money to you." He held high the wood and lead fragment once more. "I have cut the coffin up into these handy pieces, which you can purchase for just fifty dinars of gold. Take it home, bury it under the floor of your house and soon money will start to come your way. Old debtors that you thought to never see again will show up and pay in full, with interest, all they owe you. While those you are in debt to, will forgive all that is due them. Each and every one of your investments will turn a profit. Gamble and you will win. Dig and you will find gold. I predict that within a year of purchasing one of these coffin fragments you will be numbered among the rich."

If this guy had shown up in our village trying to sell stuff like this I would have marked him down as a sham huckster. However, this was not our village green, this was a magician's fair and you didn't cheat magicians with impunity. *The stuff must work,* I told myself. Still, I have enough money that I felt no need to purchase a piece of the witch's coffin.

Never-the-less a couple listeners raised their hands, indicating an interest in buying a section of the coffin, but the old man waved the away. "Not yet," he told them. "I have other products too show you first. Then you can decide which is best for you.

"So then, next I have something even more remarkable to show you. When I opened Messala's casket I found that the whole inside was a tangle of spider web. In one spot the web went round and round forming a tunnel that went down into the old sorceress' mouth. There between her skull and jaw was a nest and in the nest was a metallic blue-colored spider. Apparently the creature had been inadvertently closed up in the coffin with Messala when the lid was sealed. For two hundred fifty years the blue spider fed on the remains of the sorceress, reducing her to just bones and a few tawdry scraps of flesh. The spider tried to escape when I opened the coffin, but I caught it and you see it here in this bottle."

So saying he held up a corked beaker in which was a spider about the size of the palm of my hand. It shined in the sunlight with a silver blue color. Many ohhs and ahhs sounded from the crowd as they looked on. The spider, however, paid no heed to the crowd that was gawking at it, but rather busied itself, its legs working feverishly, in a vain attempt to climb the sides of the beaker.

"Can you imagine the power that must imbue this creature, it having nearly picked clean the bones of the great sorceress?" the wispy haired man asked. "I have no idea myself of its abilities, but illustrious magicians such as yourselves can no doubt put such a creature to wondrous usages. I ask only a thousand dinars of gold."

I had not noticed Nosdab in the crowd before the stage, but I recognized him as he stepped forward, indicating an interest in purchasing the spider, but like the last group, he was waved back by the old man.

"I have a final wonder to tell you of, then we will open for business. As I said, the coffin was completely sealed. This kept out things that normally aid in decomposition. Because the coffin was lead lined and sealed, it also kept in the natural juices of Messala's body. Trapped, they collected in the bottom of the casket. When I opened it there at its base sloshed a good two gallons of fine corpse liquor. I collected it and put it in these small stoppered bottles. Think of it, The Great Messala, she and all her great magical abilities distilled into this fine golden seepage. Admittedly, the liquid smells awful, but that, I believe to be indicative of its potency.

"Rub a drop on a sore and it will be gone within a day, rub it on a wart or mole, and two or three days will see the thing fall off. Goiters may take a week. Do you suffer looseness in the bowels? A drop on the tongue will prove quite costive. Another dram in your wine will aide in digestion.

"But aliments are not all this elixir is good for. Messala was an insatiable lover. Known for her promiscuity. Men hungered for her. It is said when she tired of a man and cast him aside, many killed themselves, saying a life that did not include her hymeneal love no longer interested them. That powerful female essence is still here in these very bottles." He held one up.

"Do you have an old maid sister or daughter? Even an uncomely one? I do not care if she is walleyed, lacks teeth, and her head is covered with wens. Let her but rub some of this magical corpse liquor between her breasts and she will suddenly have suitors by the dozen, and all offering you a generous bride price. The applications of this product are boundless. And I am asking only one hundred dinars of gold per bottle.

"So then, that concludes the items for sale today. Tomorrow, in addition to what you have just seen, I will be offering Messala's skull. Doubting not that many will want the skull, we will auction it off to the highest bidder. Think on that and husband your money for tomorrow.

Finally, the rest of her skeleton I have ground into a bone powder, portions of which you will also be able to purchase. Another reason to save your money. Do you have an enemy you want cursed? What more powerful weapon could you have to sprinkle upon, around, or poison them with, than the bone powder of such a powerful wizard. They will practically shrivel away before your eyes."

At this point my grandson turned to me and said, "I think a bottle of that corpse liquor might be a good thing to have, grandfather. Its uses seem abundant. My health is good, but I could possibly use it as an attractant to draw comely young maidens to myself."

"Just so," I declared. "Yes, I think we'll buy a couple," I told Angwyn. "A bottle for you and I might find use for one myself. Well actually it would be for your grandmother. You see, in her old age, while she still loves me, she is no longer driven by lust towards me. Our interludes of connubial bliss have become rare. However this liquid, infused into a warm oil and poured into her ears as she sleeps, might prove aphrodisiacal in its effects. At least one can hope. And, well, if nothing else at least her warts should drop away," I told him as I stepped forward to make the purchase.

With each of us now in possession of a bottle of the corpse liquor we again wandered the fair. The next booth to catch our fancy was that of a Doctor Fedellis, a seller of medicines, especially for those with bad knees. Unlike the previous booth, with a large tent and the drummer boy, this one was a brightly painted wagon out in front of which a young boy stood on a stump and played a fairy flute while a pretty, similarly aged girl encouraged three cats to dance to the music. I found the girl and cats pleasant and stopped to watch.

The cats proved equally adept at waltz and polka, and I wanted to stay and see what other dances they had learned, but Angwyn was impatient to move on, and since both of us had good knees, rather than wait for the proprietor and his medicines, I let him lead me away.

Our wanderings shortly brought us to a booth run by a toothless old hag. She was bone-thin and her clothes, while at one time very fine, were now not much more than faded rags. Her hair was dirty, and matted with dead leaves as if she had spent the night under a tree and had taken no care to clean herself upon rising. She had no tent for her booth. Not even a chair. Just a board laid between two rocks that served as a table on which she displayed five black stones about the size and shape of peach pits.

"What are these?" I asked her as I picked one up and looked carefully at it. Upon closer examination, the black seemed to be translucent and I could see that a purplish light glowed deep within.

In a voice crackling with age she told me, "What you hold in your hand is the brain stone of the arch demon Kark. These others before you came from other demons. They belonged to Mordry, Dordon, Affelance, and Xemonades."

"Their brain stones! Not something the demons would part with willingly, I'd guess."

"True, true. I did not acquire them from the demons without a fight."

"You? Fight demons!" interjected Angwyn. "An old crone like you couldn't fight a three legged rat."

She drew herself up. "Not now. I am old. My potions and my spells no longer work. I am but a shell of what I once was. But there was a time when demons cried, wept, begged, and hid in hell's innermost ring hoping Beelzebub himself would protect them from me. In those days I was known as Frenella the Diabolist. The five demons I just named, as well as others, either served me or I took their brain stones. A process that they were loath to undergo, for removal was invariably fatal to them.

"Alas, now I am old, my powers gone, and I eat only what I can grow or snare. Then one morning, not so long ago, while contemplating my garden and the day's toil ahead in it, I decided, why should I go hungry when I still have these five valuable stones. I can go the Magician's Fair and sell them and eat many months on the proceeds. I might even grow fat again. So then, for the right price I will part with one or more of these stones."

I nodded sagely, not wanting her to realize I knew nothing of brain stones. "I might be interested in purchasing one," I told her. "Which is the most powerful?"

"Depends on what you want to do," she said. "All have power over the dead. The one you hold, Kark's brain stone, can make the dead speak. Tap it three times on the deceased's right ear and then twice on their mouth and then ask them any question. They must answer and do so truthfully.

"Then this stone belonged to Affelance," she said pointing at another. "If laid in the eye socket of one who has been dead less than a year, it will allow you to see what the dead one saw during the last five minutes of life. Judges find such brain stones very valuable in murder trials."

"I heard of a man who could make the dead dance." Angwyn said. "Might he have had a demon's brain stone?"

"You can rely on it," the old hag told him. Such is the power of Xemonades' stone. Rub it on the legs of a corpse and they will fairly jump up to perform a hornpipe or if a lady is close by, they will grab her and dance a pavane.

"As for the stones of Mordry and Dordon they are like Kark's but less powerful. They make the dead speak. However, the lifeless body may become surly and resist answering questions or tell a falsehood if they do. Still the last three stones have value and if nothing else can be the source of shock and/or jocularity at wakes and funerals."

Thinking knowledge is valuable, much more so than dancing or playing tricks, I asked her, "How much for Kark's brain stone?"

"It is a powerful adjunct. He was known as Kark the Compelling, and none could stand before him until he ran afoul of me and I took his stone. For his I am asking four hundred fifty dinars of gold."

"Four hundred," I countered.

We eventually settled on a price. Four hundred twenty five dinars went into her hand and the stone in to Angwyn's pouch. My heart was full as we walked to the next booth. I had gotten my grandson a valuable appurtenance he could put to great use when he became a magician, and at the same time I had made an old crone's existence easier. If she spent the money I had paid her with care, she would not go hungry for a long long time.

We continued to wander among the booths but saw nothing else of interest to us. Evening was coming on. Looking around I saw that about half the spaces were occupied and of those most were already closed for business.

"Tomorrow at noon, as the sun goes through Equinox the fair will open again," I told my grandson. "It will be the big day. All the spaces will be filled and each of the vendors open for business. But now I've walked enough for one day. Let's go back to the inn. What I need is to sit down to some good food and fine drink."

* * *

We returned to our room in the inn and finding its other two occupants still inside, I asked them if they'd care to join Angwyn and me as our guests for dinner. They said they would, and a few minutes later the four of us were shown to a table in the inn's taproom. This large space took up most of the inn's first floor. It had a lofty ceiling held up by huge age blackened beams that crossed it every few feet. Plastered walls, with high windows, contained frescoed scenes every few yards. While these paintings depicted some wildlife and domestic scenes, most images were of a sexual nature. Not a surprising development when one has a faun for innkeeper. I mean, what else should one expect? Still… Well call me stuffy or blame it on my advancing years if you like, but I found the illustrations rather tawdry.

Angwyn, however, exhibited a wide-eyed fascination with them. Ah, to be young again when such paintings would set the heart to racing.

Who knows, if I were forty years younger, I might at least have found them educational. As it was, I maneuvered the seating at our table so that Angwyn was placed with his back to the wall, so he would have the least advantageous view.

The floor of the taproom was covered with straw. Every few feet stood a table, about half of which were occupied by other guests of the inn, enjoying their supper and washing it down with huge flagons of mead. Some guests must have been at it longer than others for they were already singing in high voices that set the hounds, which patrolled the room looking for scraps, to howling in accompaniment.

The food and mead were as good as Fynbar said they would be and he served them in more than ample quantity. Soon my belly was full and my head light. Finding my tankard empty, I raised it on high for one of the serving wenches to see as she walked back toward the kitchen. She, however, gave no sign of having noticed my raised cup.

"That girl is a bit on the lazy side," Turi told me. "I am here often, and getting her attention let alone another beaker full can be about as easy as teaching a troll to sing."

While I had food and drink in front of me I had been content to keep my peace and devote myself to them. Now however my food was gone, and the mead I'd drunk had loosened my tongue. I took advantage of the opportunity to learn more of my roommates. "Let me properly introduce myself," I told Turi. "I'm Garth Reese of Pembroke Village, and this is my grandson Angwyn. We are here for the fair. Is that also what brings you to the heart of the Goblin Woods on the eve of Spring Equinox?"

"Yes."

"You say you're here often. What is it that draws a man into such dangerous precincts on a regular basis?"

"I deal in the secretions of the Wolfsbane blossom. A foul and poisonous alkaloid to men like you and I, but to fairies it is nectar, the very drink of the gods. They add a drop to their wine and are transported in ecstasy while imbibing it. While some wolfsbane grows here in the Goblin Woods, it is of inferior quality. The best comes from Aquitaine, and it is that which I import and bring here to sell. As for danger, well, the fairies so value my trade that they have put a protective spell over me. Trolls, ogres, nymphs, and the like leave me alone for fear of the fairies' wrath that would befall them if something bad were to happen to me."

Turi leaned closer and in a conspiratorial tone said, "If you look carefully out of the corner of your left eye and towards the chandelier in the center of the taproom, there on its top you might see a small sprite sitting astride a dragonfly. One of them is always watching over me. If anything threatens me they immediately fly off to warn the fairies."

"Fairies will be here, at the fair then?" I asked.

"Of course."

"I do not wish any dealings with fairies," I told him. "They are a capricious lot. I do not like them and they do not like me. I avoid them whenever possible."

"You've had a bad experience with them, I take it?"

"Yes," I said and paused thinking back over the years before going on. "Some time ago now, a fairy king attempted to perform a transformation on me. He was foiled in the attempt and his whole kingdom changed instead. Now all their kind hold a grudge against me."

"A whole fairy kingdom, you say? In that case The Amulet of Miraculous Reversal and the words, 'dung beetle' come to mind," said Turi.

"Yes," I said. "It was long ago and is not something I wish to discuss." (see *The Poop Story by Tom Baldwin*)

"Well you have nothing to fear from them tomorrow," Turi told me. "As you must know, since you are here, a truce exists, a pax if you will, that includes all of Goblin Woods. It lasts for three days before and after equinox so that anyone who wishes to do so, might visit the fair in comfort and safety."

"True, it is that assurance that got me into the woods again. My grandson here wishes to become a magician." I nodded towards Angwyn who in turn smiled at the merchant. "We hope to find him some help in this ambition tomorrow. Possibly a mage who will apprentice him."

Turi leaned closer, once again taking on a conspiratorial manner, "As a matter of course I looked over the list of those who like myself will have booths at the fair tomorrow. With the exception of Doctor Fedellis, only a few minor magicians are listed. So unless it is Fedellis you deal with, beware of any of them offering your grandson an apprenticeship. They will take your money but have little to teach. Still, on the other hand, some of the better magicians and necromancers may be here to shop, looking to purchase some magical adjuncts. One of them might be amenable to taking in your grandson. If you like, you may check with me before finalizing any arrangements."

"Thank you for the advice. I will keep it in mind."

I then turned to the older man. “Sir, I know your name, Nosdab, but nothing else of you. Will you tell us of yourself or are you a private person?”

“I have no secrets,” Nosdab said. “I have traveled here from the fifth planet of the star Achernar. When Jupiter and Achernar and your planet’s moon form an equal lateral triangle in the sky, portals open between our worlds. There is a nexus not too far from here in the forest. I used it to be present at this fair.

“And my reason for attending? It isss simple enough he said, the alcohol beginning to effect his speech, at home I am called Nosssdab the Desultory. A name I find displeasing. I have come here hoping to add to my trunk, already full of magical items and tomes, a few more articles with the magical propertiesss necessary to effect a change in how I am perceived. Then tomorrow I will return to Archernar and my home planet. There with the help of my purchases I hope soon to be known as Nosdab the Prodigiousss.”

“For instance, earlier this afternoon I purchased a powerful adjunct, a sssspider that fed on the body of a witch. When the fair opens in the morning I will add more items to my collection then return to Achernar in triumph. But enough of this talk of me. This drink you call ‘mead’ is quite refreshing. Let me buy all of us another tankard of it.”

Perhaps the alcoholic beverages of the planets surrounding Achernar are not as stout as those of Earth. Possibly Nosdab just couldn’t hold his liquor. Regardless, as can be expected of a man in his cups, he was soon laughing and joking at things that really weren’t that funny. His eyes seemed unfocused, his speech became more slurred. However,

Nosdab was a happy drunk so nobody seemed to mind and more mead was ordered.

Having finished off two beakers and while awaiting the third he first fished in one pocket of his gown and then another as if looking for something. While he searched he told Angwyn, "Never you worries about becoming a magician. I did it. So can you. A bright boy like you just needs the proper books and tools." Then seeming to find what he was searching for he pulled out a clear cylindrical jar with a cloth secured to the top to let in air. In the flask was the blue metallic spider that we'd seen offered for sale that afternoon.

"Oh, then, you bought it," Angwyn said. "We saw you at the yellow booth where it was for sale. Grandfather bought me a vial of the corpse liquor they had."

"Yesss," Nosdab said. With difficulty he went on, the alcohol rendering his speech thick, his tongue not quite able to get the words right. "Thass where I got it. When I get home I will sssanalyze this creature and learn waysss to use it against those who don't respect me. When put to use, this ssspider alone might be enough to earn me the deference I am due."

"I respect you, spider or no spider," Angwyn told him.

"Would that all were like you my boy," Nosdab struggled with the words. "Then I would not have had to make thisss journey."

With an unsteady hand Nosdab held the container aloft. "Look how the light shines off the creature," he said.

The spider was indeed beautiful, its carapace a stunning metallic blue. Yet it was sinister too. It seemed to exude an evil presence. I would not want to own such a creature.

"I sssee fear on your face," Nosdab told me. "Know that my enemiesss at home will fear the spider too. They will flee like ssstarvelings from it presence"

He held the bottle as high as he could, next he stood on unsteady legs, one arm against the table for support, the other holding the spider even higher. "See how it…," he started, but losing his balance never finished the sentence. Trying hard to keep his legs under himself he inadvertently dropped the beaker with the spider in it. It crashed to the tabletop, broke into a hundred pieces and the spider was free. Turi, Angwyn and I all jumped to our feet and backed away. None of us wanted a thing to do with the creature.

Nosdab, however, bravely or foolishly, we will never know which, reached for the spider before it could run off. Grabbing it, he cupped it in his hands.

"Quick," he told Angwyn, suddenly sounding sober. "Empty one of the mead beakers so I can put the spider in it."

My grandson did as instructed, pouring the mead out on the floor, then gingerly setting the flagon in front of Nosdab. It was not to be, however. When Nosdab opened his fingers to put the spider into the beaker I saw it lower its rear and raise its front end before striking down, sinking its fangs in Nosdab's hand.

The magician from Achernar howled like a lost soul and flung the spider away. It hit the table hard, bounced across it and onto the floor where it lay stunned. Nosdab looked at his hand and shrieked. I could see that in just the seconds since the bite it was already starting to bloat and a webbing of black vein-like lines moved up his arm. The poor man gave out a third cry of pain that sounded like the bay of a hound on the scent and then sank to the floor.

Thinking only of saving others in the taproom from a similar fate I grabbed the flagon and bent to smash the spider under it. It, however, had recovered enough to run up the dress of a witch sitting at the next table. She must have been completely absorbed with what was happening at her own table, not to have looked around to see what had the man at the next table screaming so. At any rate, I do not think she was aware of the spider on her because she did not react to its presence until it reached her neck and repeated the rocking motion I had observed when it struck Nosdab. The bite, when it came, got her instant attention. Just as Nosdab's cries were dying down, hers rose in a crescendo of ululations as she instinctively swatted the insect from her neck and back onto the floor.

Still on my knees, for things were happening so fast, I raised the goblet once more to smash it down on the spider. Before I could the woman fell howling and thrashing on top of me. By the time I got out from under her the spider had run out of my reach and across the taproom floor. I rose and dashed after it.

As I drew closer, another of the Inn's guests, a giant man with, I would guess, a good percentage of troll's blood in him stood and attempted to stomp the spider. His foot was raised over the creature when I saw a green light emanate from the spider's eyes. The ray of light transformed into what appeared to be a green icicle or shaft of glass the tip of which pierced the sole of the man's shoe and emerged through the top of his foot.

This sent the man hopping and bellowing across the room. Me, I came skidding to a stop just a few feet from the spider. What I had just seen was magic. No spider should have such abilities. It must have absorbed more than the witch's body. Maybe, on some level, she still lived within the creature. I knew at least that I no longer wanted anything to do with the spider. The creature was more than some insect to be destroyed. Let the wizards enjoying a meal here in the taproom deal with it. I was done.

Maybe the spider recognized me from moments before, with the flagon raised to smash down on it. Maybe it was just lashing out at anyone or thing it felt threatened by. I will never know. I do know that it turned to me. I seemed to see hate in its hideous black marble eyes. Then those black eyes changed and glowed green. I do not know what plans the spider had for me. Another spike? I can only guess, for the instant its green light glinted in my direction my Amulet of Miraculous Reversal flashed in response, a ray of red light leaping across the space between the spider and I, there to dissolve the insect into a puff of blue smoke. This happened so fast that I don't think anyone else realized what had occurred, except me and the spider. The smoke floated there a few moments then drifted across the taproom as a wisp of blue vapor.

The azure cloud glided across the floor until one of the hounds that wandered the taproom came to investigate. It sniffed, drawing in the smoke, went suddenly rigid and fell over dead. The smoke drifted back out of the dog's nostrils and again the small cloud moved across the floor until it came to a wall which it rose up. Then it exited the inn through a window, not to be seen again, at least by me.

I breathed a sigh of relief as the smoke disappeared. Once again my amulet had saved me from the magic of someone or thing that had attempted to use the supernatural against me. I'll admit I was a little shaken up as I returned to our table. There Angwyn sat on the floor with Nosdab's head in his lap. I could see that the man from Achernar was *in extremis*. His eyes were focused on nothing in the taproom. They looked out over eternity instead.

Angwyn tried to get him to drink a little mead but he refused it. He did, however, give my grandson his attention for a little while. "You are the one who wants to be a magician. See what such a desire has gotten me. Yet a little while now and I will know the cold, dark, dankness of a lonely tomb. I know my fate will not deter you, but let it at least caution you. Be careful."

He was quiet for a while, given to thoughts of home and childhood I would guess, for when he spoke again he said to Angwyn, "You are kind to hold me so and comfort me in my last few moments. My mother used to stoke my hair. Would you do that for me?"

Angwyn did as the magician asked, continuing as the man's breathing became more and more labored. Just at the end he roused himself one last time to tell my grandson, "For both your kindness and your desire to be a magician I bequeath to you all that I own in this world. You will find it in my trunk. The key hangs on a chain around my neck. When I am gone take it." And so saying he *was* gone.

All this, from the moment the spider escaped till Nosdab passed over only took a few minutes. It was just as the magician breathed his last that Fynbar, the innkeeper, arrived. He had been busy in the inn's kitchen and came as soon as he heard of trouble in his taproom. He found two of his guests dead. The witch, having been struck in the neck instead of the hand, had died first. On top of that, he had a third guest cursing and yowling in pain. The noise level rose in crescendo when someone tried to draw out the spike that impaled the troll hybrid's foot. In some manner the blade had attached itself to his flesh and could be neither drawn out nor pushed on through, and attempts to do so only resulted in renewed agony for the poor halfling.

"Oh, this is a tragedy," said Fynbar as he looked over the scene while he wrung his hands. "Such a tragedy. It has been many years since anything like this has happened in my inn. Now I must hire an undertaker and deal with people's effects." He gestured to the bellowing halfling, "That one will insist I pay one of my magician guests to draw out the barb. Such a tragedy."

I looked at him and shook my head. He felt no one's pain but his own. "I will see to having Nosdab buried," I told him. "He was a stranger when you brought him to our room, but he was a friend when he died just a few hours later. Any undertaker you hire to deal with this poor woman, send them also to me and I will make Nosdab's arrangements."

"That is very kind of you sir. The gods smile on such altruism and I am sure this Nosdab will be ready to speak well of you when *your* time comes. When life is over, and we all go before the judgment bar to find out our fate in the next life, it is good to have someone already there who can give us a good character reference. For instance, I anticipate many of my former guests speaking up for me. Telling of my generosity and thus easing my way past the pearly gates." He paused for a few seconds then went on in a more business-like tone, “There is an undertaker in a nearby village I have had dealings with before. I will have him come to your room, if that is convenient. I will also have one of my men collect this Nosdab’s trunk.”

“That last item won’t be necessary,” I told the innkeeper. “The trunk now belongs to my grandson. With his dying breath, Nosdab made Angwyn his heir.”

“What is this you say?” Disappointment sounded in his voice. Then, “How am I to know this is factual and not something you just made up.”

“It is true,” offered Turi. “I, myself, can vouch for the verity of his statement. Nosdab became fond of the boy over our meal, and then as he lay dying gave all his worldly goods to Angwyn.”

“This is highly irregular,” Fynbar complained. “I normally take the effects of those who die while a guest in order to satisfy their bill. Anything left I try to return to their families.”

I knew that Fynbar’s “Anything left” would amount to nothing. That he would discount the value of whatever was found in Nosdab’s trunk to exactly equal whatever the man owed him, only to sell it later at a huge profit.”

I put an arm around his shoulder as if to console him. “Fear not, I will pay the dead man’s bill,” I told Fynbar. “In the morning present me with an itemized accounting and I will make it good. However,” and here I paused before going on in a stern tone, “be warned, do not attempt to inflate any charges or you will get nothing. You are within your rights to recapture anything owed you, nothing more.”

While this conversation was going on a man in the worn but serviceable costume of a magician stood listening. He now approached me. "Nosebad and I were old friends. I do not have a strong box like him. Therefore, he kept a number of items in safe keeping for me. Let us go to your room and open his box; I will identify for you such parcels and oddments as he was holding for me. The rest of whatever is in there will, of course, become the property of your grandson."

"Yes, we should take care of that right away," I told the magician. "The dearly departed would not want his good friend to go any longer without the benefits of his possessions. Especially a friend who does not even know his name. It is, of course, Nosdab not Nosebad."

"You doubt me sir?" said the magician. "I am wounded."

"Yes," I told him, "but 'doubt' is too kind of a word. 'Loathe' might better describe my feelings. You are just a low life charlatan attempting to profit from another's misfortune and at my grandson's expense. You will have nothing from the trunk of Nosdab unless you can produce a detailed and itemized list of what is yours before we open the chest."

He drew himself up. "I will have the law on you." He turned to Fynbar, "Innkeeper, call out the constabulary. What's mine is mine. I will not be thwarted."

"The law will not be necessary. Nosdab will tell us the truth of your claims," I said.

"How? He is dead," the magician said.

"Angwyn," I asked. "Do you have the Kark's brain stone with you."

"Yes, Grandfather."

"Do you remember how the old crone told you to use it?"

"I paid close attention."

"Good, make Nosdab speak."

Angwyn hesitated. I could tell wanting to be a magican was one thing, actually performing magic was another. And then there was handling a dead body to consider. Something I doubted he had done before. However he took a deep breath, and then did as the old lady had instructed. A few seconds later the corpse shuddered then groaned.

I bent over and spoke to it. "Nosdab, It is I, Garth."

"Speak, for I hear."

"Good. I am sorry to drag you back when you just crossed over."

"Worry not. I fear the grave. Find excuses to call me back often, even after I go to that place."

"Nosdab, this magician," I turned to the shabbily dressed mage, "What is your name."

"I am Icundis." As he spoke his name I could see he was looking around as if seeking a way out. However, he went on, "Some call me the Mirthful Magician."

I spoke again to the corpse. "This magician, Icundis the Mirthful, who cannot remember your correct name, claims to be your friend and says that in your trunk you hold certain items belonging to him. Can you speak to the veracity of these claims?"

"Yes, I know of him, but only by reputation. He is said to be a blackguard and a thief. He lies. I have nothing of his. I call on Fynbar to whip him from the inn."

“This is good advice,” said the innkeeper. “Already two guests lie dead, and a third injured. I cannot abide thievery too. Kosbert! Loswig!”

Two of the inn’s burly workers stepped forward. “Yes, Master Fynbar,” one said.

“Take this Icundis, lash him well, at least thirty times with the black whip I keep behind the bar, then turn him out into the night. That done, collect his belongings from his room and throw them into the latrine ditch.” Fynbar then looked at Icundis with the same loathing I felt for the man and said, “Should he complain about his treatment, throw him into the ditch too.”

Dispite Fynbar’s warnings, Icundis loudly protested the injustice he felt was about to be visited on him when the two grabbed him and began to frog march him from the inn. “So then, it is not just a whipping; you fancies the joys of a dip in our ditch too?” one of the men ask him.

“If it is stink he likes, he’ll not be disappointed,” said the other.

When Icundis was out the door and his outcries no longer to be heard, I turned to Fynbar again. “This has all been very troubling for myself and Angwyn. We will retire to our room now. Please have the undertaker here by early morning. I wish to settle up Nosdab’s account with you; make arrangements for his funeral and be on my way soon after breakfast.”

* * *

Back in our room, we opened the trunk of the late Nosdab. Mostly it contained books on magic. They were numerous and the titles varied, but they covered a cross section of the thaumaturgical arts. These overjoyed Angwyn. Taking a few into his hand, he said, "See, here is one on spells. Oh, and this one is on enchantments. And here, a book on controlling demons."

That latter one I would have immediately burned, but I kept this thought to myself.

"I can study these and learn much." My grandson said, his voice coming in excited gasps.

The trunk also had dozens of bottles and vials. Some held powders, others liquids, while others still had what appeared to be desiccated insects and toads. All were labeled, in archaic-looking runes I did not understand.

"Best not unstopper any of those until you know what you are doing," I told him. "Magic can be dangerous for the uninitiated."

"Yes, and I guess I will have to teach myself to read runes too," Angwyn said.

It wasn't too long until we had all these books and bottles spread around us on the floor. Still the trunk held one more mystery. Its right rear quarter was boarded off from the rest. Small wooden walls and a top forming an enclosure. The wall to the front had a hasp and hinges that appeared to allow one to open it.

"What can be in there?" asked Angwyn.

"I do not have any idea," I told him. "However, I feel caution is indicated. Magic may be involved. Since I wear and am protected by the Amulet of Miraculous Reversal, it is best I be the one to open it." So saying, I waved my grandson back then gingerly took and turned the hasp, thus opening the enclosure.

The inside was like a miniature jail. Stout iron bars separated the enclosure from the rest of the trunk. In essence, what was revealed was a small prison cell, and it was occupied. Inside was what I recognized as a cockatrice, and having done so, as fast as was humanly possible, I slammed the boards that enclosed the cage back in place.

"What is it?" Angwyn asked.

"Cockatrice." I said. "They'er small, but they're very dangerous."

"I never heard of one," Angwyn said.

"They are a hybrid creature with the head, neck, and legs of a rooster. Their body is that of a snake, and they have bat like wings. However, it is their stare that is dangerous. Locking eyes with one will result in the instant onset of a cankerous death. The body breaks out in boils and carbuncles from head to foot. It is invariably fatal."

"Where do they come from," my grandson wondered.

"It is said they are hatched from a cock's egg, on a dunghill, by a snake. This one could be valuable. There are very few in existence due to the scarcity of cock's eggs."

"But if it is so dangerous, maybe we should kill it," volunteered Angwyn.

"They are very hard to kill. In fact, the only known way is with a mirror. If they lock stares with their own reflection that will prove just as fatal to them as it would to us. Their other vulnerability involves weasels. Weasels are immune to their stare, attack and kill them on sight, and then consume their livers, which they apparently find quite nutritious .

Angwyn got up to pace the room. "I do not think I want it," he said.

“You may be right. It might be best to get rid of it. However, it is safe enough in the cage and can’t harm you unless you lock stares with it.”

“Oh, I won’t,” he told me.

“Good, and I am thinking of something I saw with a falconer once. It was a hood-like affair that they put over a falcon’s head, covering its eyes and keeping it calm until it is set loose to hunt. Something similar placed over the cockatrice’s head could protect others from it stare.”

I then took hold of the hasp that held the wooden cover over the cage in place. “Okay, Angwyn, I am going to open this again. I want to make sure there is no way for it to get out. Remember, do not, whatever you do, do not look it in the eye. Got that?”

* * *

“Who are you?” It asked in a high piping voice once I had the cover removed. And then without waiting for an answer it said. “If my master, Nosdab, finds you rifling his trunk it will go bad with you. He knows many spells. The most recent miscreant he caught burgling this trunk was last seen fleeing across a field pursued by bears.”

“Alas,” I told the cockatrice, “Nosdab is no longer with us. A spider witch stung him to death. This is Angwyn,” I nodded towards my grandson. “It is he who is your new master. Treat him with respect.”

Before the creature could respond, Angwyn spoke, “Why did Nosdab keep you confined in this cage? What did you do to annoy him?”

"I did not 'annoy' him. It is in my power to grant wishes. He kept me that he might exploit my abilities. For instance, as a display of my powers, if you set me free, right now, I will give you both wealth and twenty seven beautiful virgins." Then, as if assuming Angwyn's acquience, the cockatrice went on, "Do you prefer blondes? Dusky temptresses? Auburn beauties? Or if you prefer I could arrange a mix."

"Listen not to him," I counseled Angwyn as we stood with our backs to the cockatrice. "Do nothing hasty. Promises are cheap. His ability to deliver the women is open to question. Study your books first, then when you are in a position of strength deal with this creature."

Angwyn sat deep in thought for what seemed a long time.

"He is trying to tempt you," I told my grandson. "The possibility of obtaining a superfluity of money and women, is a Siren's song that has drawn to many men to their undoing. Do not join them."

"I won't grandfather," Angwyn said. "I will study as you said. I will learn to control, not trust this creature." To the cockatrice he said, "You may yet earn your freedom, but it will be on my terms. So then, for now we will close you up in your cell."

"Wait," the cockatrice cried, but I paid it no heed and shut up its jail once more.

* * *

Morning found me paying our tab and Nosdab's with the innkeeper. I then purchased a fine casket from the undertaker, contracted for a church funeral with a minimum of two priests and twenty wailing mourners to follow the body from village to burial ground, and arranged to have a fitting memorial carved to sit atop his grave. After that we loaded our trunk and Nosdab's on our mule and headed for home.

As we left I looked around for Icundis, fearing he might blame us instead of Fynbar and Nosdab's ghost for his troubles. He was nowhere to be seen however, and for this I was thankful.

Our trip towards home was a quiet one. Angwyn was lost in his thoughts and plans. He only emerged from them a few times and each one he thanked me profusely for all the help I had given him these last few days.

The sun had just set when we finally emerged from Goblin woods. Instead of trees the road now ran between farmer's fields green with the approach of Spring. Ahead glowed the lights of a village. "That is Evening Borough," I told Angwyn. "They have a fine inn that spreads a good table. There we will spend the night."

Feeling the content of Nosdab's trunk was valuable beyond words I only got one room. Angwyn and I would sleep in shifts guarding it. Not wanting to leave the trunk even in a locked room we took it to our evening meal with us, leaning it against the table as we ate.

The taproom was noisy, as most are. The evening crowd filled it. Wine flowed freely and with it came drunken song. There was even a fight. I paid it all no mind, and instead concentrated on reducing the chicken I had been served to a pile of bones. Were we home and this our village inn I would have gladly joined in the drunken revelry. But not here. I wanted only to retire to our room with its locked door.

I had just finished my meal and was busily sucking grease from my fingers when a horrible smell engulfed me. It was as if I suddenly stood atop the village dunghill. I nearly gagged.

"What the…" I swore looking around. There behind me stood a man covered in what looked and smelled like sewage. It took me a moment to realize it was Icundis.

My eyes must have gone wide with the recognition for he said, "Yes, it is I. Did you think to deny me without consequence."

"But the pax. You cannot disturb us going or coming from the Magicians Fair."

"It only holds within Goblin Woods. What happens outside the forest is of no concern to those who maintain the peace that surrounds the fair. Here, you have no protection. And you will find any compassion on my part lacking."

A hand seemed to grip my heart as I realized he was right. Out here, away from Goblin Woods we were at his mercy. Knowing it was probably futile, I nevertheless tried to reason with him. "I did you no harm. It was Fynbar that had you whipped and consigned you to the cesspit and he did so at the urging of Nosdab. It is with them that you have any quarrel, not my grandson nor myself."

Icundis laughed. "Nosdab is beyond my reach and Fynbar will pay for what he has done. Someday he *will* pay, just not yet. As for you and the boy, your time is now. I have spent this whole day following you and planning my revenge. The price you will pay must be amusing. Something that will entertain people, making them laugh at you and the boy for your foolishness in attempting to thwart me. Can you think of anything like that?"

My mind churned. *I must talk him out of any deviltry, or baring that get him to use his magic on me and not the boy.*

After a pause he went on, "All this might have been avoided had you shared the bounty of Nosdab's trunk with me. But no. In your greed you wanted it all for the boy. Now he will have none. They said he wants to become a magician. Now that will never happen."

Angwyn had stood up as we had this conversation. His fists were balled and I could tell he was ready to fight. I waved him back into his chair.

"What are you going to do?" I asked the magician.

"I am not known as the Mirthful for nothing. I think a transformation is in order. People find those the most humorous, don't you think. So then the question becomes what shall you two become? The boy, I think would make a fine hedgehog. Don't you agree? He already has big brown eyes and shaggy brown hair. It will not be much of a change at all. You, however, I have puzzled over. You made some unkind remarks to me last night. You implied I am a thief. Yet you are the thief. Taking what should and will be mine. So then, I asked myself, does the animal world have any notorious thieves? And the answer is, 'yes.' And what are these little thieves? Why, pack rats, of course. So then, it is a pack rat you will become. How do you fancy a life of collecting shiny little objects for your den?"

I realized there would be no talking him out of what he planned, so I must get him to use his magic on me first. "I see now the error of my ways," I told Icundis. "However, the boy is my grandson. I could not bear to see him changed into a hedgehog. Change me first, so I can scamper away down some hole and not see him thus."

"Such sentiment is moving. However, I had already determined to change the boy first. You may close your eyes if sight would be too much for you. Do so now for I am about to affect the transformation," he said as he turned to Angwyn.

"No," I screamed and threw myself at the magician. I managed to get my hands on his throat and squeezing, stopped him from uttering the fateful syllables of the enchantment that would result in Angwyn becoming a hedgehog. But I am old and Icundis was young. It did not take long for him to pry my hands free of his throat.

"Very well, have it your way old man," he told me as I now tried to claw at his eyes. "You may go first." Then he shoved me backwards so I fell to the floor, but he did as I'd hoped and spoke the spell that would see me transformed into a pack rat. However when the last word was spoken my amulet flashed, a shaft of red light flaring from it to the magician, and it was he that began to shrink in size while at the same time his features changed, becoming more rodent like with each passing moment. Surprise, then shock, then fear played across his features as he realized that somehow, some way, his magic was transforming him and not me.

After about fifteen seconds a no doubt astonished pack rat sat stunned at my feet. I reached down grabbed it before it could run off. Other guests at the inn were gesturing and laughing at Icundis. "Well," I told the pack rat, "I see you were indeed aptly named. Even at the end you bring mirth to the hearts of people."

Holding him up I looked into his black eyes. I could see hate smolder there. It might have been a pack rat I held, but it was Icundis too. "Don't be too hard on yourself," I told him. "You are not the first to try and use magic against me and fail. For you see I wear the Amulet of Miraculous Reversal." So saying I pulled back my sleeve displaying the cause of his undoing where it encircled my wrist. "Any magic direct against me, this amulet turns back on those that would harm me."

Icundis treated me to another hate filled look while his no doubt tortured mind sought some way out of his predicament. I meanwhile, stared back at the pack rat, wondering what I should do with him. I was considering putting him in the tiny prison cell in Nosdab's trunk. He and the cockatrice could keep each other company. But any plans I might devise for him came to naught when he suddenly bit my hand. Shocked by the sudden pain, I instinctively shook it and the pack rat fell to the floor. In an instant the transformed magician was off running for the door. He never made it, however. Just as he was about to escape into the night one of the inn's cats raced out from under a table and grabbed the pack rat in its mouth. I heard a few squeaks of horror and dismay as the cat carried Icundus back under the table. The cat must have been hungry for it didn't play with its catch as felines often do. Instead it made a quick meal of the pack rat and Icundis the Mirthful was no more.

* * *

Once we'd returned to our village I found a fine stone house for Angwyn. In front ran a well maintained road while behind the house Meady Meadow, a green and grassy expanse spread across the property and down to a small lake known as Wynona's Wheary Water. The home had a large, airy workroom with a high ceiling and many windows that made it well lighted. A large fireplace kept it warm. It also had a fine great room for entertaining guests, a well appointed kitchen, and several nice bedrooms. The home seemed just right, a place where Angwyn could immerse himself in his studies of magic. Knowing the distraction the fairer sex might be to a young man, I also hired The Hag Mildred, a venerable widow even older than I, to keep house and cook for him.

It wasn't long before our village was filled with stories of strange sights and sounds to be seen and heard near the house. It also seemed that working for Angwyn was good for the hag. She was looking younger with each passing week. Villagers said Mildred seemed less wrinkled and the glow of youth was coming back to her cheeks. Some even claimed that calling her a hag no longer seem appropriate. I smiled at these happenings. Angwyn's studies seemed to be bearing fruit.

* * *

Oh, and many have asked if the corpse liquor from the casket of the arch sorceress Messala proved efficacious for my dear wife. I am happy to report that after her third dosing I began to see a marked improvement in her reception to my advances. However, a problem has arisen. When I attempted a fourth application she woke as I poured it in her ear. In her wrath she has made it clear she takes a very dim view of me decanting anymore warm oil, suffused with the corpse liquor, into her ears while she sleeps. I have to admit there is some small justification to her reaction. The corpse liquor has an abominable fetor, its miasma clinging to her for days after a dosing. However, I feel, and I think you will agree she over reacted. I mean threatening to put a borer beetle in my ear while I sleep, should I dose her again is going too far.

So, in answer to your many questions, while progress has been seen, it is arrested at least for the time being.

The Amulet of Miraculous Reversal

Or A Grandfather's Saga

The Third Tale: Ogre

It was warm for such an early spring day. I was up with the roosters. Yawning, stretching, enjoying a gentle breeze coming in off the sea. It smelled of kelp, tasted of salt, ruffled my hair. Some gulls circled overhead, their cries blown away on the wind, while the sun rose in a cloudless sky. I filled my lungs and looked around. Flowers grew in a nearby ditch, and the fruit trees bloomed in my orchard. Bees hummed, newly awakened from their winter naps, they were out hunting pollen and nectar.

I tried to take it all in, and with a smile nodded my head to no one, or to everyone. I guess to myself most of all. I couldn't help but think Spring's beauty a harbinger of better things and finer days to come.

Yet such optimism can be misplaced. In fact, it amazes me how fast things can go from good to bad. One moment it's light, the next dark. One second life is sweet, the next bitter. Would that the opposite were also true. However, when things are getting better, they always seem to take a while doing so, the change gradual, a process. Yet dreadful drops on you like a boulder.

That day was a case in point. Afternoon found me sitting with some of the other elders of our village. We'd gathered as usual on the veranda that runs along the front of The Inn of the Red Tusked Boar, a clapboard structure in need of whitewashing. It serves as the gathering place for our small village except Sundays which finds us in church instead. Whenever the weather is fine, you can locate us graybeards out there, sitting in the sun with tankards full of the innkeeper's ale. We pass the time taking turns telling tales (with the occasional embellishment) of our younger days and past exploits. It was, after all, as good a way as any, to keep ourselves occupied until heads started to nod as the time for our afternoon naps approached.

As I recall, Berwyn the Tailor had paused in one of his rather Scheherazadean confabulations to wet a dry throat. Such pauses were frequent when Berwyn was pitching a tale, for he was a tosspot of renown, and it didn't take too many words to parch his throat and make his elbow bend.

It was as I watched Berwyn's adam's apple rise and fall with each gulp of ale that I heard a child's voice calling for help. I looked towards the sound and saw young Lodrun running up the dirt road that bisects our village. Lodrun, a thin boney boy of about eight, was out of breath, his gait not the light footed run you would expect of a youngster. Instead it was a thumping clumping effort of one trying to overcome exhaustion and keep moving in spite of muscles that cried out for rest. I saw, too, that his clothes were torn, and his arms and legs were cut and bleeding as if from forcing himself through hedges and thorns.

Seeing the child like that, a coldness gripped my heart and I knew of a surety that something bad had happened. It was with a feeling of dread that I rose to my feet and ran out to meet him. He fell into my arms. I held him up and said, “What’s the matter, boy?”

“Ogre,” he said. Just that one word: “Ogre.” But it was enough. Our bright spring day was suddenly as dark as midnight. The sun might be warming my skin, but I felt a chill grip my heart.

Ogres vary in size and ferociousness from land to land and kingdom to kingdom. I know not what your experience of them might be, but let me tell you our island is home to some of the worst. Here they grow to nine feet tall and are as heavily muscled as a Greek God. Their skin, a mottled gray, is covered with warts, and wattles. Their wide shoulders are surmounted by three heads, all atop long hideous necks. They have wrinkled faces, splayed noses, bloodshot eyes, and huge fangs. Each head has a separate personality, but they share in common the body of the ogre. How this is accomplished, I do not know.

While nature would seem to dictate that there must be female ogres somewhere, the ones I have seen have only been male. A fact they poorly disguise with small dirty loincloths.

“It took my friends,” the boy sobbed.

Between hiccups and tears, shivers and nervous glances over his shoulder, I got the story out of him. It seems that Arianell, who taught the seven and eight-year olds at our community's school, had taken her class out into the fields to collect wild flowers. Before you condemn her, know that it is only on very rare occasion that creatures of the haunted woods venture forth on to our farmlands. Our village is also many miles from the woods. So, we do not live our lives in constant dread of the beasts of Goblin Woods.

It seems that as the class ventured along the narrow neck of land between Wheary Water Pond and Ethelred's Mire, suddenly the birds ceased their singing and even the insects went silent. Instead strange noises and rustlings came from behind a nearby tree. Frightened, the children dropped their flowers and gathered near their teacher, all except young Lodrun who instead ran towards a brambleberry thicket where he hid and watched.

It is good that he did, for only from him did we find out what had happened. As the children bunched together around Arianell, and stared frightfully towards the trees, there suddenly appeared a great round net such as fishermen toss. It spun across the sky to settle over the little group. Almost before they could cry out in surprise and fear, the ogre bounded from behind the trees, reached under the net, pulled Arianell out, threw her to the ground, then beat her again and again with a huge cudgel he carried. When the teacher's cries ceased, the ogre tossed her lifeless body into the mire.

Next the ogre drew the children one at a time from under the net and put a kind of wooden yoke on their necks. These he tied all together.

When the last child was secured, he folded his net and by means of a long rope dragged the young ones off across the fields and towards the road that ran to Goblin Woods.

"Tell me," I demanded when he'd finished his story, "My granddaughter, Rachel, is in your class, what happen to her?"

"He took her with the others."

"No," was all I could say as I looked away from the boy trying to imagine a world without Rachel.

My beautiful little grandchild carried off by an ogre. I couldn't wrap my mind around such a concept. What horrible fate awaited her? Usually children taken by ogres were eaten quickly, but some were kept alive, to work as slaves for the beast, taking care of his house, gardens, and livestock. Neither destiny was one I cared to contemplate for my Rachel.

I realized at once that we had to get up a band of the village men and take after the beast. It would not be hard to find willing members for this posse either. With what I would guess was ten to fifteen of our young children carried off, the men and especially the fathers would be clambering for rescue and revenge.

I knew too, that I would join that band. Not just because one the children carried off was my granddaughter. My little Rachel! That would be *my* reason for going. However, there would be another reason I would go too, that being the village would want me to go along even though I am old, and my strength wanes. They'd want me for the simple reason that I am the one villager with at least a little magic.

Most people around here know that that for decades I have worn The Amulet of Miraculous Reversal. For those that don't, it has been mine from the time I took it from the desiccated corpse of the Arch Mage, Rhialto the Forlorn. Since I first put the amulet on, it has protected me from any magic directed against myself.

It possesses great power and turned every member of a fairy kingdom into dung beetles when they tried to transform me into one. A mountebank of a conjurer named Claractus the Climber no longer has legs of flesh and blood, instead he must get about on a pair of black chitinous fly's legs thanks to my amulet. And one must not forget the sorceress Malloqu who tried to use magic to spread lies about me and my family. She now sports a forked tongue nearly a foot and half long with which she constantly tests the air in a snake-like manner.

Few people outside our village are aware, but in addition to my Amulet, some years ago I obtained a Contract of Service for the demon Raushan. It constrains him to obey the contract's holder until he has worked off a total of ten indenture points.

With the pact came a magic flute with which I summon the demon when his services are needed. Raushan always arrives reeking of sulfur, in a foul mood, unwilling to cooperate, and all the while making horrible growls and outcries instead. I realize I shouldn't allow such insolence, but I haven't been too hard on him, because, in a way I think I can understand his surliness. Are not the circles of hell said to be an unpleasant abode at best? Dwelling there for eons could very well result in even the most endearing individual developing a sour disposition. So, for the most part I let him alone, summoning him rarely and then mostly when parents come to me complaining of naughty children that need to be scared into behaving.

* * *

It only took us about an hour to gather a posse of local men and set out in pursuit of the ogre. There were ten of us. I brought the rusty old, but sharp sword I owned. Of course, I wore my amulet, and hoping I might find some use for it, I brought along the flute that summoned Raushan as well as the indenture that gave me, its holder, power over the demon.

The others were armed with swords, and spears. One man brought a morning star. I nodded with satisfaction when I saw it. Its spiked iron ball on the end of a chain, when swung with authority, could crush even the bones of an ogre like an eggshell. We also brought food and bed rolls if night should find us before we caught up with our adversary.

Things went well, and we made good time. The trail left by the ogre and our children was easy to follow and headed straight towards Goblin Woods. We'd assumed that would be his destination, and his tracks confirmed it. That forest is the haunt of various magical creatures, not just ogres, but trolls, ghosts, fairies, nymphs, as well as magicians and sorcerers. The ogre would be going as fast as it could make the children walk, for it had to know that if a enough of us caught it in the open farmlands that surround Goblin Woods that by sheer weight of numbers, we could probably kill it. However, once back in the forest and in its lair, it would be much safer from us.

We made good time and trusted we were going faster than the ogre since he could only go as fast as the children. This was confirmed by those of our posse who had tracking skills. They told us that we were catching up and that another hour should see us overtake the monster.

Ogres are not particularly bright, but he had to understand that taking our children would result in a pursuit. He also had to know that the shortest and quickest way to the woods was across the Marasmic River. This can only be done by ferry, as the river's waters are infested by tanatoid eels that will swarm on and in just minutes skeletonize any creature that enters the water. If we attempted to wade or swim across, none of us would make it. So being the cunning devil that he was, and knowing we must use the ferry, the ogre saw to it that we couldn't.

We came through the trees that line the river's course to find the ferryman dead, reduced to a bloody pulp by the ogre's cudgel. The rope used to pull the barge like ferry from a dock on our side of the river to one on the far side had been cut on this side and now dangled from the far dock a hundred feet away and impossible to retrieve. The large flat-bottomed ferry itself was nowhere to be seen. The Ogre probably used it and then let it loose to drift away on the current.

There were other ferry crossings up and down the river, but the closest was six miles north. To go there, cross and return to the trail would cost us at least three hours. We would not be able to take up the ogre's track again until nearly dark and would surely lose it in the oncoming night's gloom. We'd be forced to wait till morning to continue our pursuit, which meant we could not catch him before he had our children deep into Goblin Woods.

A terrible gloom settled over the posse. We knew starting out that catching the ogre and retrieving our children would cost us some lives, but now it looked like most of us would not return. Fighting the ogre in his lair would be so many times more dangerous than here on open farmlands. What were we to do?

Then an idea came to me, *What about Raushan*? With his powers, it would be, but a few moments work to set the ferry to right. Yet it was not something he'd do willingly. There'd be hemming and hawing to listen to. However, with the fate of my grandchild hanging in the balance, I was in no mood for his surliness. He would do as instructed or face my wrath. I retrieved the flute from my pouch, told all the men to move back about fifty feet, and played the tune that summoned the demon. He wasn't long in arriving. He'd appeared in various guises over the time I'd possessed the flute. This day he chose his favorite, or at least the one he used most often, that of huge thick bodied black lizard some twenty feet long with smoldering skin that gave off a sulfurous rotten egg smell and orange eyes that seemed to glow from an inner heat. As usual he was in a foul temper, his long tail lashing in fury, and he immediately produced a series of hideous groans and growls.

"Quiet," I demanded in a loud stern voice.

Shocked, he cease his cries. Raushan seemed a little surprised at my tone but recovered quickly. "And why should I?" He demanded right back. Then looked down as if peering into the earth's bowels and the very heart of perdition. "What have I done to deserve such a fate?" he asked. "Why must I, an arch demon, heed the demands of these short-lived little creatures? Their lives are like the blink of a firefly on a summer's eve, one moment there and the next gone. I have lived two eons and I am but a middle-aged demon."

If he awaited a reply, it was in vain. None came. So, he looked up, gazing into my face, "It's an outrage that you can tell me what to do. Were you some mighty or magical creature of the forest, strong and terrible, and asking evil deeds of me, I would not be so resentful of your commands. I might even enjoy carrying them out. But to obey the whims of a mere man, bah."

Up until now I really hadn't been bothered much by his truculence. I'd purchased his indenture and the flute on a lark, with no specific goal in mind. Commanding a demon had seemed like it might be fun. When it wasn't, I moved on to other things. But now I was desperate. We had to get across the river and do so quickly. I would not give in to his bluster as easily this time.

Now, as you must know, demons are powerful creatures, but not very clever or intelligent. I would make it simple for him. "You will do as I say because I hold your indenture." At this his tail lashed even more furiously, his back arched and he hissed. But I just I held up the sheet of paper. "See here where it says for two pounds of gold you will do as the indenture holder asks until you have worked off ten points. And there," I drew his attention to a scorched area of the document. "There is where you made your mark. Of those ten points you still owe four and a half. Today you will work off some of that obligation."

"But…" Raushan started to say but I interrupted him. "No 'Buts,' I am in haste. You will do as you are told."

"You must understand," the demon wrung his forepaws, "I was under pressure. Mine was not an enviable situation. I had gambling debts that needed to be cleared away. Being a debtor is not an admired trait even in the infernal regions. Beelzebub does not tolerate it. And so certain, shall we call them 'collection agents,' pursued me. I had to pay or else. A broker agreed to give me the two pounds of gold I owed if I signed the terms of indenture. Were I not under duress I would not have consented to ten points for only two pounds of gold."

I tapped my foot in impatience and Raushan paused a moment, his eyes looking into mine in a vain search for sympathy. However, he did not give up and went on, "So in all candor, I think you should forgive the remaining four and a half points. After all, you are an old man. Your appointment at hell's gate cannot be far off. An act of altruism such as I just suggested might earn you favor and even a better placement. In fact, I could whisper in certain ears, find you a spot in one of the outer rings. It is said to be much cooler there, and the smoke not nearly as bad, nor does the brimstone rain down so heavily. Why, after a few millennia, you might come to think of it as almost balmy…"

"Enough, enough, spare me." I interrupted the demon. "As I said there is need for haste. First, the only gate I intend to approach after this life is pearly, and second, I will not give you points. You will earn them. You will earn them starting now.

The demon did nothing, just stared at me.

"I am losing patience and you will either do as you are told or I will call for an arbitrator. When I tell him of your stubborn lassitude, he will no doubt issue me a persuasion rod. A few stokes with it will bring you to heel, and see you springing about with great vigor in your endeavor to obey and thus forestall the next application."

"No, please, not a rod." I could hear the fear in his voice.

“If you force me, what other choice have I?”

Raushan said nothing for a few moments, then a grudging, “Very well,” but I could see resentment burning in his eyes.

Ignoring his rancor, I went on. “Now here is what you shall do. See how the ferry across the river here has been vandalized by an ogre? You must travel down the river and find the ferryboat and return it here. Then you will repair the rope that runs from side to side of the river and put all things back to right. When you have done all that I will strike off a full point on your indenture.”

“Only a point, I thought two or maybe three.”

“You jest,” I said. “It will be but a few moments work for you. But I am in a hurry and prepared to be magnanimous for some quick work. So be off. I am waiting.” Once more I could see resentment on his face but only for a moment because Raushan had disappeared.

The other men of the posse cheered when the demon was gone. We all thought we would be on our way again quickly. It was not to be, however. Time passed and the sun had dipped close to the horizon with no sight of him. Finally, around a bend in the river we saw the ferryboat returning. It was being drawn by what appeared to be two small knights riding ponies. Raushan floated in the air above. Seeing him lazing there I blew a summons on the flute.

“Why have you taken so long? I thought I made it clear that haste was in order.” I demanded of him.

“A difficulty arose.” He seem nervous as he went on, “I found the boat about a mile south of here, but the ogre had stove in the underside so that it had taken on water and eventually sunk to the bottom of the river. I could not go in after it. All my skin would peel away.

"Know you not that we demons are allergic to water? Even our magic cannot penetrate water. Seeing the boat there, knowing I was helpless to raise it myself, and wishing to avoid having you vindictively lay about me with a persuasion rod, I knew that I must use my wits if I were to achieve the ends you desired." He paced about a few moments then said, "I knew I would need magic other than my own if I was to please you, so I flitted to Goblin Woods and began a search. It took a long time but finally I found what I sought, a troll in close proximity to one of the fairy kingdoms that dot the woods.

"I took the form of a voluptuous fairy princess with flowing green hair and wearing a diaphanous gown that set off my buxom figure to good effect. Then I wandered close to where the troll hid in a thicket. As I had hoped he jumped out and grabbed me. I must say, my screams of fear and anguish were most piteous. The troll, however, was not moved to mercy, and having torn away at my clothes, was preparing to abuse me when two fairy knights that had heard my cries came riding to the rescue." Raushan stopped and looked at me, maybe looking for approval. I just tapped my food in impatience.

"Seeing the knights," Raushan told me, "the troll took off running but their horses were swift and rode him down. One fairy knight put his lance through the evil creature's back. This must have been quite painful as it induced a great deal of screeching and thrashing about by the troll before the second knight's lance pierced its heart and put finished to he who would have deflowered me. The knights then came riding back in triumph, each holding high one of the troll's ears. Their disappointment knew no bounds when they found me instead of a princess waiting for them.

The demon paused in his tale to gesture to the two fairy knights who were now drawing close with the barge in tow. "I captured these two and their horses and brought them all to the site of the sinking. You see, while their magic is not as strong as mine, it can penetrate water, and so I made them raise your boat, heal its wounds with fairy stuff and tow it back here. Now I will have them repair the rope and reattach the boat. When they have done that, I'll turn them free, and you, you must give me the point I have earned."

* * *

I could have sworn I saw a smile on Raushan's face after I signed off a full point on his indenture. I thought to see it just before he disappeared back to whatever inner ring of hell he called home. But then, well, maybe I didn't. I mean can a lizard smile?

Regardless, we'd lost over an hour-and-a-half in getting over the Marasmic River. Now dusk was coming on and a deep malaise gripped my soul. The ogre had gotten away with our children. It would be suicide to enter or wander about in the Goblin Woods after dark, when the malaroids come from their caves to hunt and ghosts walk the darkness. All we'd accomplish would be providing them with a meal. We were going to be forced to wait until morning to enter, and the trail could have gone cold by then.

The other men of the posse were even more depressed than I. More than a few were cursing, and a pair even began to fight. And why shouldn't they? What had any of us to look forward too? First a sleepless night on the ground, followed by a perilous search of a malignant forest where we might or might not find our children, but would surely find danger.

Well, I thought, I *can at least do something about that sleeping on the ground part.*

"There is a village about two miles to the north, I've never been there but have heard of the place." I told them. "It lies on the edge of the woods. So come, rather than the dank earth I will pay for all of us to sleep in comfortable beds. I may die tomorrow, you may die. At least let's spend our last night in a proper bed. I have more than enough money to pay for this, and it is what I want to do. Besides, a good night's sleep will see you a well-rested warrior. We must all be at our best tomorrow when we fight the ogre."

The logic of my argument was obvious to all and we began to trek towards the village. As we drew close I noticed a farmer in a field next to our road, who having unleashed his horse from a plow was leading it in the same direction we were going. His clothes were dirty and perspiration stained. His hair he wore in greasy spikes. As I neared him I detected the rank odor of stale sweat and saw that his skin was greenish in tint with a dusting of scales on his face that increased in number to a solid mass by the time they passed down his neck and below his shirt. *A halfling*, I thought. *Mostly human, but someplace in this man's family tree lurks a mermaid.*

"Ho, friend," I addressed him.

He stopped and turned an appraising look on me. He did not seem pleased with what he saw and said, “I am content with myself and my life. I am in need of no aphrodisiacs, unguents, gout curing distillations, seepages, and hair restoring salves. My movements are regular and suppositories unnecessary, nor do I desire pain-relieving elixirs. That being the case, I suggest you take your business elsewhere.”

“No, wait,” I told him. “We are not merchants. I do not wish to sell you anything. I seek only your wisdom. I need some advice.”

This aroused his interest for he said nothing, but turned an inquiring look on me. It would seem he was loathe to part with his coin, but might make free with his counsel.

“You see, good sir, we are strangers to these parts and were wondering if we might be well received in the village yonder. Customs and beliefs vary from place to place and we have no wish to offend out of ignorance.”

His look left me and traveled over my companions. He took a fair amount of time appraising them before announcing, “Our village is called Saskervoy. We normally welcome visitors so long as they are well-mannered, deport themselves with gentility, and do not offend our sensibilities. However, I must warn you, philistines such as yourselves will not be received with joy.”

“Philistines? We are simple village folk such as yourself.”

“Are you? We are modest folk and consider wearing one’s doublet open at the collar quite barbarous. No person of refinement would do so. Yet I notice at least half your number have chest hair showing. Quite uncouth, I must say.”

I turned to the others of our posse. “Everyone, secure your doublets all the way to the top.”

When all had done so I said, “There good sir, you see how easily we become civilized?”

“What of him and him,” the halfling exclaimed as he pointed to two of our members. “They wear yellow. Yellow is a color all Saskervites deplore. It is only donned by men preparing to do harm or murder another. And that one over there,” he pointed again, “He was looking me up and down with the calculating and avaricious glare of a tax collector. How can we welcome such to our village?”

Thinking fast I said, “Customs differ. In our village a man displeased with another dons orange garments, that the person might see and mend their ways. Yellow is instead the color of sanctity and these two wear it in hopes of inducing god to bless our cause. Still they will take off anything yellow. As to the last man’s stare, he is not a tax collector, but a conscientious and dedicated coffin maker and embalmer and was no doubt just sizing you up for one of his caskets. Notice the rings he wears in his ears. Are they not sphincter clamps kept at the ready should an opportunity present itself? No tax collector would sport such adornments. Life, as you must know, is fleeting and the poor fellow just strives to be always ready should a need for his talents arise.

“And for you,” I told the farmer, “being so magnanimous with your advice, I feel sure, by way of thanks, he would extend your family a discount should something happen to you.”

"Saskervoy has its own undertaker," said the farmer. "He is a man I wish to avoid the attentions of for as long as possible, and even more so, those of a foreign grave digger."

"Quite so," I told him. "It is an appointment we all wish to forestall. Still, do you not see that we are very inoffensive and only wish for a good meal and soft mattress?"

"Well," the farmer allowed, "I guess you might take lodging at the inn. But be warned, the rates are dear. Oh, and a bit of advice. The innkeeper's wife is a very irritable witch. Anything she asks, do it. Anything she wants, give it. Her fuse is short and her anger burns hot. Those that antagonize her learn to regret it. Now I must leave you. Here is the way to my home." And with that, he turned up a narrow lane and left us.

The inn, being the only two-story building in the village, was easy to find. It stood among squat red brick homes that lined either side of the street. All were built to the same pattern. Two windows with a door between.

The innkeeper, one Xexanmendes, was a corpulent man with splotchy hair worn short where it still grew. I could see that Xexanmendes was also a halfling. This time I thought to detect troll in his linage and was not surprised. Trolls are known for their insatiable sexual appetites and care little, with what or with whom they couple. Hence their spawn is common enough along he fringes of Goblin Woods.

When I looked at the others of the community who had come to the inn for dinner it soon became obvious that this was in fact a village of halflings. Troll and fairy blood seem most common among them. For others, I could not put my finger on their antecedents. Whence comes black fur over the entire body, or eyes on stalks?"

I haggled little with the innkeeper. Food and rest were important, money not so much. I had plenty. So, I hemmed and hawed only enough so he would not take me for a fool. When the bargaining was over, he led us into the dining area. It was a large room with an aisle down the center. At least a hundred candles burned to give it light. I was surprised to find all the locals crowded on one side of the room. On the other, the tables were empty except for one person. What appeared to be an older woman dressed in a red tunic and a red cape and cowl sat alone sopping up drippings from her plate with a crust of bread.

All the seats on the other side of the dining area being already taken up by what I assume were locals, the innkeeper led us to the empty side and said, "Normally, this half of the dining area is dedicated to the sole use of my wife, Scarlotta. However, business is brisk this evening and we must set aside custom, so then if you will find yourselves seats on this side of the hall, I will see about getting your meal served."

Soon our tables were creaking under the weight of the food on their tops. The aromas of roast fowl, fresh bread, and sweet wine filled my head as I ate, and I must say the innkeeper spread a fine meal. We all ate heartily.

While we were eating, I reached for a squab from a platter some distance down the table from where I sat. Having grown up in a large family I was used to reaching for what I wanted. Proper manners were maintained, or so I had been taught, so long as a single foot remained on the ground while stretching out for food, and I'd just managed to keep one there as I went for the bird.

While doing so I felt the hairs on my neck rise and knew I was being watched by someone. I peered around to see who was looking at me and saw it to be the innkeeper's wife, Scarlotta. It was not me violating some local custom by reaching, or not asking to have the birds passed that had her attention, however. It was my Amulet of Miraculous Reversal. As I had stretched out for a squab my sleeve had pulled back revealing the bracelet like amulet where I wore it on my wrist.

I normally kept it covered in order to avoid envious stares and the unwanted attention of footpads. There were, however, instances like this when I inadvertently revealed it, and now she looked at it wide-eyed with surprise. Her head and neck bent back in awe of my bracelet like-amulet, thus letting me see under the cowl she wore. She was old with wrinkled dark pink skin, red eyes, and red teeth.

"That bracelet you wear," she told me. "The gray metal it is made of is old, thick and ugly, but the red stone mounted on the top is wonderful. I must have it."

My Amulet of Miraculous Reversal is indeed made of a gray metal, a metal that burns with some inner fire and is always warm to the touch. The surface of the amulet is incised with runes. I have asked several magicians to read them for me, but all say the writing is so old that knowledge of the runes' meaning have been lost in time.

Surmounting the amulet is a large red stone about the size and shape of a half walnut shell. The jewel seems to tap the amulet's inner fire for is glows with a radiance that is not so noticeable in daylight, but after nightfall or in a darkened room is obvious to all. Scarlotta was not the first nor did I think she would be the last, to be attracted to my amulet by the beauty of the stone that sits atop it.

"I am sorry," I told her. "The amulet has been mine for many years and I am loathe to part with it."

She stiffened when I spoke, and her hands clenched into fists. "Let me tell you something of myself," she said. "I see the world as being divided in to two camps, one peopled by those who please me and the other by those who don't. The ones with whom I am pleased know me as The Crone Scarlotta, a magnanimous older woman who collects trinkets and other objects of red. Those with whom I am displeased know me as The Red Witch who takes whatever red items she desires and leaves behind some awful bane that will serve as a warning to others who might deny me. Now then, how will you call me?"

"Well," I tried to sound calming, "a woman of your beauty should be known by neither the ugly sobriquet 'crone' nor the even more pejorative 'witch.' They both have revolting connotations, which must never be applied to a lady such as yourself. I think I'd prefer to remember you as an interesting woman with whom I shared a drink. Will you not join us? Sit here beside me and fill your trencher from this jug of fine wine."

Yes," she smiled. "I will join you, but first you must ask the gentleman next to you to eat elsewhere for I see yellow fibers on his clothing and find that color deplorable. Oh, and of course you still must give me the red babble on your wrist. Do those two things and I will gladly join you."

"The wine, yes, this I will give you, and my company also, I will share," I said. "However, my amulet has protected me these many years. It I must keep. But see here, my cape is secured by a large red pin. It is yours for the asking."

Her expression darkened. "Enough of your evasion. Will you or will you not freely give me that red object I glimpsed at your wrist?" Her hand made a grasping motion but I ignored it as she went on, "I saw it but for a moment, but the red, oh the red. It captivated me. Nothing in my collection is its equal. I must have it. So, will you give it or must I take it?"

"I cannot let you have it." She was asking more than I was willing to give. I wanted no trouble, and had no idea of the strength of her magic. She might be able to take it. But if so, that was the only way she would get it, for I would not give her my prize possession I thought of calling up Raushan, but there was no time. Things were coming to a head fast.

She paused a few moments, seemingly lost in thought. Then she nodded to herself and said, "Prepare yourself for a favorite spell of mine. First conjured by a magician named Ludwig over a century ago, it carries his name to this day and is called Ludwig's Loose Limbs. It changes your bones to jelly. In but a few moments now, you will lie shapeless on the floor begging me to take what I want and restore you. Take I will but restore I won't. Your friends will carry you around in a basket for the rest of your time here on this plane of existence."

"Wait," I cried. "Don't…"

I never finished the sentence. Red fire seemed to flash from her fingertips and reach across the room for me. Before it reached me, however, my amulet flared. Her red fire turned to yellow and curled back on the witch. She let out this horrible sounding scream such as only an old woman can make as the flames engulfed her. Then she tumbled to the floor. For ten or fifteen seconds she writhed there while her clothes wisped away and her skin blazed. Then suddenly the fire died out. It was just gone! There was no smoke or smell of anything burnt. It was as though the fire had never happened.

The posse members stared from her to me and back to her again in amazement. They had all, no doubt, heard of the workings of my Amulet of Miraculous Reversal, but never thought to see it in action or behold some evil creature's magic turned back on its source. In this case, Scarlotta did not seem to have been physically harmed in anyway, nor had her bones been turned to jelly, for she held her shape well. However, her red clothing had burned away. She was totally, completely, absolutely, stark raving naked as a jay bird, nude. For this reason, I and everyone else in the room could see that Scarlotta's skin had changed to the color of lemons. Only her eyes, her hair, and her nails were different. They were now a yellow orange.

It took her a few moments to recover from the shock of being enveloped in flames before she realized that she had been changed. The puzzled look on her face changed to horror. It was not the horror of being naked in front of a crowd. It was the horror of realizing she and everything about her was now yellow. She let out with another of those old woman's screams of anguish then asked what I had done to her.

"I have done nothing," I told her. "Your own avariciousness has led to your present sad state. I tried to warn you, but you would not listen." I pulled up my sleeve so she could clearly see the bracelet I wore. "This 'red bauble' as you called it is the Amulet of Miraculous Reversal. It turned your own magic back on you.

"The amulet imposes its own brand of justice. It also has a sense of humor which I doubt you see, however I can detect it in your case. You," I made and expansive gesture, "and your whole village have evidenced a great distaste for yellow, and now you are yellow, a yellow I feel sure will not wash off. I suggest you turn from your evil ways and learn to love yellow, the color of sanctity. Cease being the Crone this or the Witch that and become instead… instead… wait, wait…, yes I have it. You can expiate your sins by instead becoming the Saint Scarlotta. A simple but virtuous woman who ventures into the haunted forest to clothe the trolls in yellow and teach them to sing."

I could see she didn't think much of my suggestion, but I am used to that. My very own wife rarely listens to me, let alone obeys my orders.

I shrugged my shoulders and returned to my meal, reaching out once more for a squab. It was as I was finishing the last of my ale that the innkeeper ran forward and handed Scarlotta a blanket to wrap herself in. He then turned to me and not surprisingly went back on his offer of sleeping accommodations after what had just happened to his wife.

Luckily we found the year's first cutting of newly mown hay in a field just outside the village where it had been gathered into a number of haystacks. The posse and I spent a comfortable night within the soft warmth of the hay and all woke rested and as ready as possible for whatever the day held.

* * *

I was surprised at the ease with which we found the ogre and our children's tracks that morning. I had expected them to be lost amid the trails and marks of the forest's night creatures. But they weren't and by mid-morning they had led us to a huge old wooden pile of a fortress that the ogre called home. It might have at one time been beautiful, but no more. The grounds had gone to weeds, boards hung loose from the walls, and portions of the roof lacked shingles. It had a general appearance of disrepair.

Yesterday's events had set me to thinking as we followed the ogre and our children's trail. Scarlotta's fate had given me an idea that might get us back our children without the need to take on the ogre in his own den, where any fight would favor him.

As we stood at the great wooden gate of the ogre's stronghold I called the posse about me and told them, "Before we storm this bastion I want to see if may haps I might be able to make a deal with the ogre for the return of our little ones. I want to see if he might trade them for Raushan's chattel. The demon is willful and rebellious, as you saw yesterday, and of little use to me. However, who knows the value an ogre might put on controlling such a creature? So, let me go in there and see. If you do not hear back from me within an hour you will know I am dead, and you can deal with the situation however you deem best."

A few minutes later, with the men of the posse hiding and watching from behind nearby trees, I raised and let fall a huge knocker on the door of the ogre's home. I soon heard the scrapping sound of a key in a lock and then the door squeaked and creaked on rusty hinges as it was pulled back by an elf.

"What do you want?" the repulsive creature asked. Elves are notoriously ugly, but this one took the cake. His sickly gray skin was a battleground where warts and moles multiplied and spread in an endeavor to see which could cover the largest area. However, what really took my breath away was the vile stench that wafted out the door to engulf me. It stunk mostly of death, but there were hints of decay, mold and rodents. It was so bad I was awhile recovering before could I answer. Finally, I said, "Yesterday the ogre that lives here stole a number of children from my village. I came to get them back."

"Oh, wants them back, does you? And why should my masters care what you wants?"

"Normally, I do not think he would. However, I have an offer to make he may find tempting."

The elf leaned forward and took my forearm in his hand and squeezed it in testing manner it a few times. "'Tis you they may find tempting. Old folks, they can be tough and gristly, but I expects you would tender up nicely in a stew."

I jerked my arm free from his hold. "Beware, I have certain magical abilities," I lied to the elf. "I know a few incantations. For instance, are you familiar with Septicus' Curse of the Bubbling Bowel? Those who have experienced it, could they rise from their chamber pots, would warn you to caution." I then pulled at my chin in a contemplative manner while I looked him up and down before nodding and going on,

“Or since you already have a profusion of warts it would take less effort to transform you into a toad. So now, announce my presence to your master and do so quickly or you will spend the rest of your days in a stagnant pond pursued by storks.”

My lie had its intended effect. The elf became suddenly solicitous. “Now, now. No need to be that way,” he shrank back. I could see fear on his face. “Yesterday was tedious for the masters. They are having a late breakfast. If you will follow me, they can receive you in the dining hall.”

The passageways of the ogre’s castle were dark, and dank. The occasional candle lighted our path and the horrible smell only grew worse as we progressed. I could hear nothing except the sound of our steps on the naked stone flooring and the rustling and squeaking of rats or mice that fled before us by the dozens as the elf lead me through the keep’s cavernous depths. Finally we came to a huge dimly lit room. Age blackened beams held up a high ceiling. Rows of tables and chairs occupied the main floor, Here and there, along the walls were propped up a couple score of suits of armor, all broken and smashed. Trophies, no doubt, from knights that had come here to rescue maidens or children over the years. At the end of the room one huge table stood perched on a raised dais and there the ogre sat eating his breakfast..

“Masters,” the elf addressed it as he led me down between the tables and toward the ogre. The elf seemed to puff with pride and get back his bravado as we approached the dais. “I bring you what I hope may provide a few moments entertainment and then this evening’s meal.” He stopped and turned an appraising eye on me. “I was thinking a hearty ragout with lots of onions to kill the rancid flavor these old ones have. Of course, that is but a suggestion. It is for you to decide. Just let me know when you finish with him."

I ignored the elf and approached the ogre. I hoped my baggy pants concealed the fact that my knees were shaking violently. The suits of armor along the walls had convinced me the only chance our children had was for me to actually pull off my plan involving Raushan. The men of my village would not be able to defeat the ogre by means of arms. The smashed armor decorating the hall spoke to this monster's martial abilities.

"Oh great ogre," I said as I gave a humble bow. "Forgive my informality. I know not what to call you."

"You may call me 'Zot,'" the leftmost head spoke while waving about the enormous leg of some creature, probably a troll. Having given its name Zot then took a huge bite from the leg. "And I am Zam," said the middle head. Finally the right one said just one word, "Zim."

"Sirs," I said while giving a second bow. Straightening up, I went on. "Yesterday, you took a dozen children from my village. I am here to purchase them back."

"We have no need of gold," said Zam. "We place no value whatsoever on it. What we appreciate is a fine meal, and more than that an excellent banquet. For this latter reason we took your children. You see, Zot here is about to fall. When that happens we will hold a great feast for all the ogres of the forest. Your children will provide the main course."

"Bah," Zot interrupted. "I will not fall. I have sent down tendon and sinew deep into the shoulder below me. I will hang on many more years before I fall."

"This is wishful thinking," said Zam. Then to me, "Notice the bulge on our shoulder next to Zim. A new head is ready to erupt. So, it goes for us. Every fifty years the leftmost head drops away while a new head pokes from the right shoulder."

"Bah," Zot said once again. "I will not fall."

"You will fall, and soon. Then we will have a banquet to honor our new head, Zil. The invitations to the party have already gone out. I sent them when I started to feel the new head gnawing at the skin and trying to break through. Surely you must sense it too."

"I feel it. I ignore it. Our skin is tough, its teeth small. Much time remains before it erupts."

"Must you two squabble in front of this man thing? It is undignified." Zim said in a loud voice. "By dinner tonight Zot will be no more. His head will lay in some corner, or under a table, his face frozen in a look of surprise. And you, Zam, you will be eating this very creature you now let listen to your personal arguments with Zot. So, stop I say."

"Bah," Zot said. "I tell you I will not…." But he didn't finish the sentence this time, for he was interrupted by a sound, like a stretched out bow-string being released. His eyes went wide as I heard more reports. Snap. Snap. A pause and then another Snapping sound. Then finally a particularly loud crackling reverberation was followed by Zot making a gasping sound and then falling head and neck from his perch on the ogre's shoulder to bounce across the table and then off to the floor where he landed with a thud and rolled into a corner just as Zam had predicted. At almost the same moment the skin on the Ogre's right shoulder split and a new head poked forth.

Watching the new head look quizzically around while Zim and Zam gaped at it, I felt events were conspiring to thwart any chance I had of saving the children. I tried to seize back the initiative. "Master Ogre, I feel privileged to be here and to have witnessed this momentous occasion in your life. However, just before Zot fell Zim said something about me being eaten. That is not the purpose for which I have come. Yesterday you stole a dozen children from my village. As I said earlier, I want to purchase them back from you."

"Impossible," said Zim. "You saw Zot's fall. You saw our new head, Zil's, eruption into the world. Such events are always the cause of great joy and we will hold a grand feast for all the ogres of the forest to celebrate. Your children will provide the main course at this banquet. A succulent young child makes for excellent eating. And as for you, as Zim predicted, you will provide this evening's repast."

I took a step back, a shocked look on my face. "Sir, I did not come here to be eaten, I came to trade."

"And I told you we do not value gold. The objects you man things accumulate in order to call yourselves rich mean nothing to us. You can best serve us by filling our gullet."

"Still, I thought you might value magic," I said trying to sound puzzled. "Do not all creatures value magic?"

“Say on,” Zim spoke with a sudden interest showing in his expression. In fact, I could see that I had the attention of all three heads, though the new one called Zil only looked at me with a puzzled gaze.

With a flourish I produced the Raushan’s chattel papers and the magic flute. “Sirs, with these two objects you can become the master of one of Hades’ most infamous dwellers. Perhaps you have heard of the Arch Demon, Raushan. Condemned to one of Hell’s inner rings, he is of a nasty disposition. When he rages the whole earth shakes. Yet this chattel,” I waved it. “Signed by Raushan, compels him to do as he is instructed by the legal owner of the document. And this is the flute used to summon him whenever you have a chore you wish him to perform.”

“True, he only owes a remaining three and a half points before he is free. But surely a being such as yourselves can find enough evil things for him to do while working off those three and half points to more than equal the value of a dozen small children.”

Zim turned to look at the other heads, “The man thing’s proposal interests me.”

Then he looked back at me, “But I never buy anything I cannot see. You say you can summon this demon, then do so.”

“Be prepared,” I told them before putting the flute to my lips. “He is quite fearsome.”

I should have known better than to try make them fear Raushan before he appeared, for this time he came in the guise of an effete gentleman such as frequent the king’s court. His hair was powdered white and his mustache waxed to sharp points. He had a forked beard also waxed to points. He was decked in shiny green silk trimmed with white lace that fit tightly over a thin body. He wore a large red hat with an outsized ostrich feather that curled high over his head. It would seem he'd taken extra care in developing this guise but had forgotten his feet. Instead of fancy shoes with silver buckles, he had the cloven hooves of a goat.

"You summoned, master?" he asked in a piping voice.

The two older ogre heads began to laugh, while Zil's expression just seemed confused.

"Raushan," I said. "You have often complained of serving me, a mere man. I am attempting to sell your chattel to this ogre, who is known for his strength and his wickedness. If you wish to escape my care you must impress this creature. So show yourself in your most common guise, that of the huge black lizard."

Raushan, with a calculating expression looked from me to the ogre. I saw a smile come to the dandy's lips as he gave the ogre not a bow, but an inclination of his ostrich feathered cap before dissolving into a cloud of sulfurous smoke. Then just as quickly he was back again but as the twenty-foot long black lizard. He made the usual groans and growls while displaying a red mouth full of evil looking sharp teeth.

Seeing him thus, the ogre recoiled and I thought it would run from the room, but when Raushan did nothing more threatening than growl, the ogre regained its composure and then its seat.

"There, Sir Ogre," I said. "Here you see Raushan at his worst. He is yours in exchange for the children."

Zim and Zam put their heads together and conferred while Zil just looked around bewilderedly. The two heads parted after a few moments and Zim said, “And this demon commands magical powers too?”

“Oh, yes, Sir Ogre, only yesterday Raushan captured a number of Fairy Knights and put them to work in my service. He can be very valuable. I will admit he can be stubborn at times, but the mere mention of calling an arbiter or threatening the use of a persuasion rod… Well, he comes around rather quickly in such instances.”

Raushan must not have liked the mention of persuasion rods for he let out with a particularly loud rumble.

Zim spoke again. “And you will trade the ownership of this demon’s chattel for the children?”

“Yes, oh yes. They are very dear to me. I must merely sign here,” I pointed to a spot on the paper, “This is a legal document and by signing I thus release my control of the demon, then when you sign here as accepting Raushan, you become his new master, and just like that he is yours to command. I should warn you, he will try to haggle over the price of his services, putting exorbitant values on them, and you should show a firm hand in distributing credit for tasks performed lest he take advantage of you.”

The two heads went back into consultation. When they finished Zam spoke. “We will accept your offer. As you point out, twelve children are a small price to pay for control of a demon. The lands surrounding the forest are full of children and it will be but a day’s work to collect more.”

"Very good, Sir ogre. Very good. If your servant could fetch a pen, we can accomplish our business and I can take the children home." And just a few minutes did see the transaction completed.

When we had both signed I handed the flute over and said, "Now, Sir ogre, can you have the children brought around, I wish to leave. We have a long walk ahead of us."

"You need only walk as far as our kitchen," said Zim. "Did you really think wc would honor a deal with a man thing. You and your kind are just food. We do not make deals with our dinner." He turned to Raushan, "Demon, I wish to see your powers at work." The ogre pointed at me, "I want you to destroy him."

Again I thought, *Can a Lizard smile?* It looked like that was what Raushan was doing as he stepped towards me his mouth wide. It would take him but a few gulps to swallow me whole. I backed up.

"No," said Zim. "I want to see magic. Do something magic."

When I heard that my heart skipped a beat, in fact, many beats. My plan just might work.

"Very well," said the demon. "I came to hate this man and wanted to taste his blood, but I will settle for watching it spilled." He was silent for a while, no doubt pondering Zim's demands, then Raushan said. "This time of year the woods are full of hungry bears just awakened from their winter naps. I will use my magic to find and fetch some of them to eat him."

And Raushan was gone. But then he was back, almost in an instant. Between me and him appeared two grown male bears and a large female with two cubs."

The bears lunged this way and that but some invisible force constrained them.

The ogre pounded its table in approval. "Yes, yes." Said Zim. "Hungry bears. Wonderful. It will be worth a meal to watch him torn apart, and his dried and grisly old flesh consumed by the beasts."

"And I agree," added Zam. "Despite the elf's best efforts and a multitude of leeks and onions nothing would ever make him palatable anyway."

Having been given his instructions, Raushan turned to the animals, "Bears, I have summoned you here by magic. Do my will and eat this man thing alive."

The moment I feared was upon me. I'd not expected the ogre to honor any deal we made. I'd hoped he wouldn't. I just prayed that like a child with a new toy, it would want to see a demonstration of Raushan's power and that would take the form of magic directed against me. My amulet had protected me many years from all sorts of earthly magic. Just yesterday from the evil witch Scarlotta. But was it proof against the magic of hell too? I had gambled that it was and was about to find out.

With roars the male bears charged, and I cringed, ducking my head afraid to look at those slavering jaws about to close on me. But then I felt the amulet grow almost hot to the touch on my wrist and suddenly red light struck out from it enveloping the bears like an aura, stopping them in mid charge and turning them around towards Raushan.

Then once they were turned, abruptly the red light was gone and the bears charging again, but this time Raushan was the target. They were on him in an instant, faster than the demon could dissolve itself into smoke. One male bear sank its teeth in his neck and the other his back just above the hind legs. The one with his teeth in demon's neck shook Raushan like a terrier with rat in its jaws. The other bear, putting a foot on Raushan's back to gain leverage began ripping great hunks flesh from his back and wolfing them down unchewed.

Desperate to dislodge the bears the demon tried to go into an alligator like death roll but only managed to turn himself over. This was a mistake for it exposed Raushan's soft under belly, which the two bears attacked. Raking with their claws, they tore the demon open and disemboweled him. After that the demon's fierce struggles tapered off quickly and soon ceased. Raushan was no more but the bear's feast was just beginning.

I have often noted that things have a way of seeking balance. Hades was now minus one of its own and the inner rings of hell had an opening for a new occupant, but that seat would not sit vacant for long.

The ogre, seeing how things were going tried to flee. In his panic he blundered between the she bear and her cubs. Not a wise move. With a roar of warning and rage she pounced on the ogre like a ferret on rabbit and bore him down. One swiping blow of her massive forepaw saw Zam fall. He bounced across the floor in a fair imitation of Zot, his features frozen into a surprised expression that seemed to say, "This is not supposed to happen." Then her jaws sunk into Zim's neck and a moment later ripped him free too. Zil tried to get back under the skin he had recently erupted from but it was not to be. The cubs had latched on to him. Their little bodies bounced and jerked as they wrenched and tugged until they worried him loose from his place atop a shoulder too. In all the ogre proved not even a minute's work for the she bear and her cubs. Soon they were grunting with satisfaction as they feasted as well.

The bears were too busy eating to pay me any mind as I backed quietly and unobtrusively from the ogre's dining hall and then ran from his lair. I fetched the posse from the woods. Our search proved a short one. We found the children locked in a dungeon, but unharmed.

The elf was discovered in his kitchen, hiding amongst the pots and pans he'd intended for our children. He fled squealing like a pig stuck under a gate, but we caught him and dragged him from the kitchen while he kicked and screamed for mercy. But there would be no mercy for him. He had no doubt butchered and served up children and others by the score. I did the world a service as I personally tossed him shrieking to the bears, the largest of which snatched him like a salmon from mid-air. In just seconds his screeching outcries were replaced by the sound of his bones crunching.

Once we had the children out and the now satiated bears had left the fortress as well, we put the ogre's lair to the torch. It produced a satisfying fire with a column of smoke that could be seen for miles around in Goblin Woods. Our journey home was a happy time, knowing our children were safe and that one less evil lurked in the haunted forest.

Behind us we left a sign in front of the burned-out fortress that read "Let the fate of Zim, Zil, Zot, and Zam be a warning to all who would harm our children."

The Amulet of Miraculous Reversal

Or A Grandfather's Saga

The Fourth Tale: Lust and Greed in the Woods

The summer sun was warm. I'd just returned from my daily trip to the Inn of the Red Tusked Boar. My stomach was warmed and my mind a bit fuzzy from all the ale I'd drank, but it was a good fuzz. I had a smile on my face as I pulled my chair to a spot under my cherry tree where the sun's rays couldn't find me, while the cooling breeze would. Birds sang above, their songs mingling with the cries of my younger grandchildren playing a game of ogres and goblins nearby. It being well into the afternoon and time for my nap, I sank down into my chair and dozed while my mind wandered down various paths of memory.

"Grandfather." A voice brought me back from a remembered adventure. It was my oldest grandson, Xander, named after my own father, and for both those reasons a favorite of mine.

"Yes, Xander, did you need something?" I asked him.

"I don't know," he answered. "Mom said you would want to see me before I depart."

"Ah yes, now I recall. Your mother spoke to me concerning you. You are off to the University and she wonders if you are ready. She fears you are somewhat gullible where members of the fairer sex are concerned. She does not want you beguiled or taken advantage of."

He bridled at my words "Mom worries too much. I understand girls. I know their ways and I am not as easily taken in as she seems to think."

I gestured to a nearby chair. "Sit, sit." He did so and I told him, "The female of the species is not as easily fathomed as you seem to think. They are deep and in some cases dark creatures. Their hold over men can be uncanny. We are bigger, stronger, wiser, and yet they can bend us to their will with ease. This is especially true of the pretty ones."

"I do admit a weakness were the good-looking girls are concerned," he allowed. "I get this funny feeling and just want to do whatever they ask."

"I know the feeling well, you obey in hopes of a reward: a smile, a touch, a kiss, maybe even more."

I got up and moved my chair close to his and went on in a conspiratorial tone. "I will tell you a story, one not many in the family have heard, and certainly no other grandchild of mine. It must never come to the ears of your grandmother. You must promise never to repeat it."

"You have my word, grandfather. My lips are sealed."

"Good, for it is a tale I think you may profit from it. This is the story of my second trip into Goblin Woods."

He looked surprised. "I knew you had been there once. It is where you acquired your wealth and that marvelous amulet you wear on your wrist. But I did not know you had ventured into its depths more than just that one time."

I nodded. "Yes, I have ventured into that haunted home of all man's fears more times than I care to remember. It is a bad place. In Goblin Woods each of the seven deadly sins reign supreme. You are aware of these sins?

"Rest assured, Father Ambrose has seen to that portion of my education," Xander told me. Then he recited them for me. "They would be pride, envy, wrath, gluttony, lust, sloth, and greed."

I gave him a pleased nod. "So then, in this story I am about to tell you, you will learn of my experiences with two of the worst of them: lust and greed.

"All of the family knows of my first time in that forest, and how I acquired both great wealth and my magic amulet. You already know how I got possession of a huge hoard of fairy gold and jewels. I won't bore you with a rehashing of those events. However, what I usually fail to mention is the fairy's wealth was so great that it was more than I could carry. I brought out all I could, enough to make me rich and then some, but the rest I left behind, hidden in hopes I might come back for it one day. As the years went on and my hoard of gold slowly depleted. I could not stop thinking about what I had left behind. The desire for it ate at my soul like a canker. Finally, I decided to put my fears aside, give in to my greed, and go back for the rest of the fairies' treasure. That was my first sin.

"So let me tell you of my return, or to be more exact, of my attempted return. It was a few years after my first adventure in those woods. I went back to the place I had exited the forest all those years earlier and tried to follow the trail back in. However, the further I went into the woods the less familiar things looked.

"Then I came to a fork in the road. Thinking back, I seemed to remember from my previous time in the forest that another trail had indeed joined the one I was on, but try as I would I could not recall from which direction it had joined the one I had been traveling. I peered up the path that went off to the left and then down the one that disappeared into the trees on my right. I pondered a moment about which to take."

Right has always been my lucky direction, I reminded myself. *'It won't fail me now.'* But it did. After a mile or so the path petered out to not even a game trail, and before I knew it, I couldn't tell from whence I'd come, let alone where I was going.

"This was not supposed to happen. I'd planned on entering Goblin Woods at dawn, by noon to have made my way to the meadow where the fairy castle had been located, find the treasure I'd buried there years before and most importantly be back out of the forest by evening.

"I had very good reasons for wanting to avoid those woods at night. They would include the ghosts and ghouls, trolls and goblins, as well as other assorted creatures that call that forest home. Not the sort of beings one wants to cross paths with anytime, but especially after dark. To put things in their simplest and starkest terms, I did not want the next day's sun to find me reduced to a scattering of well-gnawed bones.

"Realizing I was lost, I looked this way and that, my frustration building. Why couldn't things go as I'd wanted them to? I had tried to avoid danger, but now I was up to my eyeballs in it.

"I endeavored to console myself with the fact I was wearing my magic bracelet known as The Amulet of Miraculous Reversal. It has protected me from danger since the first day I wore it. What disconcerted me was, I didn't then and don't even now know what sort of limits it might have. I could only be sure that there was some level of protection it couldn't offer. That was obvious since I had acquired it by removing it from the long dead and desiccated corpse of its previous owner.

"Still the amulet's powers are not negligible." I held up my wrist that my Grandson might admire the amulet before going on with my tale. "This bracelet turned back the magic of a fairy king who sought to transform me into a dung beetle, changing the king and all the fairies subject to him into the noisome insects instead.

"You may also have heard of a minor magician, who has come to be known as Claractus the Climber, but you may not know how he came to be called such. It seems he coveted my amulet. However, he feared that any curse he put on me the amulet would be made operable on himself instead, and so he sought to get it from me by indirect means.

"The fool attempted to use an enchantment called Dutwiller's Sticky Feet to transform the path on which I took my daily walks down by the river, into what might be best described as a giant piece of flypaper. I was later told he had hoped I would become hopelessly stuck and give him the amulet in return for rescue, or if I refused to part with it, that he might retrieve it from my body after I died of thirst or starvation.

"Things did not work out as he envisioned, however. It seems the amulet sensed his plans for me and when he activated the enchantment instead of the trail changing to fly paper, his own legs transformed into those of a fly.

“This has not proven to be entirely to his detriment. Having fly like suction cups for feet, Claractus can now climb walls and walk across ceilings. Whole new lines of employment have opened to him. I have been told he has become quite rich working as a spy.

“Nevertheless, he is dissatisfied. Prior to the change he was known as somewhat of a lady's man, but the transformation seems to have put his love life completely on hold. The young women, who used to welcome him to their beds, now spurn him instead, finding his thin black chitin legs distasteful to view. Those nearsighted enough to be able to overlook his appearance report that the sharp stiff bristles that cover his fly legs abrade the women’s thighs, and thus they, along with their more sharp-eyed friends, now avoid any conjugal activities with Claractus. This to his great vexation.

“But, I stray from the story. Forgive me, going off on tangents like that. Happens more and more lately. Age I think.

So then where was I? Oh yes, my story. I was lost in Goblin woods and. . . Well, it was almost noon by then, what with the sun directly overhead it proved no help in determining directions. I knew my way out of the forest was to the west, but what was west?

“*Okay*, I thought to myself as I looked up towards the sun, *I'll just sit here until you move past your zenith. Doing so you will show me which way is west, which also happens to be the direction of the forest's edge. I can still be out by nightfall.*

“The air was warm, there was no breeze stirring, and a sheen of sweat covered my face and dampened my clothes. Wiping my brow with my sleeve, I sought the comfort of the deep dark shade of a huge old knurled oak that stood nearby. The tree looked foreboding, its twisted branches clawing at the sky in seeming desperation. However, the fallen leaves under it proved soft and comfortable, and once I'd settled down the forest seemed to come to life around me with bees buzzing amongst nearby flowers, while crawling insects busied themselves in the dry leaves on which I sat. A dragon fly even came to light on the toe of my boot where it sat staring at me with large reddish eyes. It was all quite idyllic until a strangely mottled yellow squirrel with disproportionally long legs discovered my presence and came to sit on a branch above my head where it proceeded to scold me for I knew not what. No normal squirrel this. I speculated that it might be another creature, that like myself had fallen afoul of the fairies these woods were rife with. They may have put an enchantment on it, but an incomplete one leaving it half squirrel and half who knows what. Studying it, I decided it reminded somewhat of an elf by its pointed ears and long nose. If it had previously been an elf, it must have been a grouchy one. For despite any outward changes it had retained that foul disposition. Irritated at its banter, I said, 'Be gone,' and I tossed a dead branch at it, sending the squirrel creature scampering up to the top of the tree.

"The noisome little beast gone, things became so peaceful I was nodding off when a sound of crashing in the undergrowth brought me back to full wakefulness. I looked towards the noise and saw a deer dash out of the trees and onto a nearby meadow. The animal paused, breathing hard, its tongue lolling out. I could see where a small arrow or dart of some kind had pierced its side and blood ran from the wound to stain its fur. The wounded animal didn't linger long before reentering the woods on the meadow's far side.

"Not a minute lapsed before more branches snapping and dead leaves crunching announced the coming of pair of trolls following the deer's trail. The trolls wore outfits of bright hunter green with yellow piping and buttons was well as red pointed hunters caps with a huge white plumes that stretched up high and then out behind at a jaunty angle. Both carried tiny bows in one hand while with the other they held a leash at the end off which struggled a scaly and blackish purple goblin imp. The imps were apparently being used to track the deer for they kept their noses to the ground. This devotion to duty by the imps was rewarded occasionally when one or the other found some drops of blood to lick from the grass, after which they raised their heads high to let out ear piercing screams of excitement.

"I froze, certain that a man would be preferable quarry to a deer, and frightened that the slightest movement on my part would attract their attention. Luckily what little wind there was, was from them to me so they would not catch my scent on the air. Still, fearing to even breathe, I watched the trolls, all the while praying that the shadows under the oak were deep enough to hide me from their sharp eyes.

"The hunting party was just opposite me when the squirrel returned and set up a racket again. With its feet, it pounded the branch on which it squatted while at the same time grunting and grunting as angry squirrels are wont to do. It was almost as if it were trying to get the trolls' attention and say, 'Look what's under my tree. I don't want him here. Do something about it.'

"My heart froze in my breast as one of the trolls turned his head to the squirrel's sounds and raised a hand to shield it eyes as it looked into the depths of shadow under the oak where I hid.

“As if encouraged, the squirrel started to make intricate signs and movements with its forepaws, as if it could cast a spell in this manner. Then it let out one more of what was going to, no doubt, be another series of barking grunts. However, before it could finish the first grunt the rodent suddenly went limp and tumbled from the branch on which it had sat and landed at my feet. It still breathed, but I could see that something had stunned it.

“With the squirrel’s cries abated, the troll turned away, giving its attention back to its lunging and tugging imp. That foul little beast, its green eyes glowing with avarice, had detected another blood stain, and it wished to get there and have the grass licked clean before second imp could arrive and share in the bounty. At the same time all this was going on I felt a warmness at my wrist where I wore my amulet. It had surely been the cause of the squirrel's timely fall. I smiled, pleased that it had again protected me, but at the same time I shook my head in puzzlement, once more unable to fathom the magical rules that governed it.

“I waited quietly under the tree another quarter hour, giving the trolls plenty of time to get far away. Then feeling enough time had passed and seeing that the sun was definitely past the zenith so that I could tell in which direction west lay; I got to my feet and again attempted to exit the Goblin Woods

“Having got my bearings I was glad to see that West was not the way the trolls had gone. I had no desire to see their pretty green outfits and red caps again, and even less desire to be pulled down by their goblin imps.

"Instead my direction of travel was almost the opposite of theirs. Unfortunately, however, my way led through heavy underbrush, and I had to force my way through tangled thorn and canker weeds, all the while hoping that I would soon find the trail again.

"After about an hour of very slow rough going, and not finding the path, I was running with sweat, my clothes forming a clammy embrace. You can imagine my joy then, when I came to a large pool of water. It was roughly circular and about hundred feet across. A drink of its water and splashing some its coolness on my face and neck would be pure heaven.

"Unlike most ponds in my experience, the water of this one was crystal clear and even though small waves rippled the water's surface and distorted my view, I could easily see all the way to its bottom where dark stones lay strewn about interspersed here and there with white ones.

"A gurgling brook found its way from among a stand of huge old black oaks to feed the pool. The water rushed over a large slab of rock that jutted out into the pool like a shelf. It was there, next to the brook that I leaned down and reached out a hand to cup some of the cool water.

You can imagine my surprise as I looked into the pool and saw a beautiful young woman looking back at me. She was about a foot under the surface and emerging from under the slab of rock I kneeled on for my drink.

"She smiled up at me, her eyes a beautiful green, her teeth perfect, her flowing hair trailing over milky white shoulders. She looked to be in her mid thirties, at the peak of her beauty and womanhood. She was undoubtedly the loveliest female I had ever seen, and as more of her came into sight I was stunned to realized that she was not wearing a thing."

This detail brought a smile to Xander's face. He hadn't seemed to interested in my tale to this point, but suddenly I had his complete attention. *Ah, teenaged boys.* I smiled to myself and made a mental note that if I ever wrote a book it would have to have a few naked ladies populating its pages, otherwise none of my grandsons would read it.

I nodded to him a few times as if to say, "Yes, you heard aright." Then I went on with my story. "I gasped in... well, in shock. But I must confess the gasp had a bit of delight to it too. As you know, women of our village, especially the pretty ones, keep themselves well covered. Our priest has taught them that such is proper, and they obey.

"Once she was out from under the ledge the lovely creature surfaced and swam to a rock about twenty feet from the pool's edge. There she climbed out of the water and reclined in the warm sun.

"Beads of water glistened on her skin like diamonds and I was sure I had never seen a lovelier sight in all my life. I couldn't take my eyes off her, she, however, paid me no heed. Ignoring me, she instead absorbed herself in squeezing the water from her long blonde hair. However, I have always been sharp eyed, and I could see that while she feigned disinterest, she was often taking surreptitious glances my way.

"*What sort of woman is this?* I found myself wondering, *And how did she come to be swimming in this pool?*

"As if in answer to my thoughts, she finished with her hair and turning to me said, 'I am Dryope, and this pool is my home. I live here with my sisters. Some call us dryads and others water nymphs or sirens. As to the accuracy of these claims, I cannot say. I just know that I love this pool, and never want to leave it.' She stopped speaking and reached to pluck a water lily, which she put in her hair to lovely effect.

"Then looking coyly at me over her shoulder she spoke again, 'My only regret is that there are no men here. This part of Goblin Woods is wild and little traveled. I grow so lonely, having only occasional visitors, like yourself.' Then after another pause and with voice lowered an octave she went on, 'I know you too will leave me, just like all the others have, for the forest is a place of danger to you.' She paused, looked about, a pout on her lips, and then heaved a resigned sounding sigh before going on in a happier tone, 'Oh, you needn't be sorry for me, though. I understand. This pond, it is my lot in life. But, first then, before you go would you come out here on my rock and hold me for a space. Let me feel the touch of a man for just a little while before you leave?' So saying she stretched herself like a cat, then lay on her side, an elbow propping her head and quietly watched me.

"Now I'd been warned by our village priest of the seductive powers of languid females. Such is, as you know, a favorite theme in many of his sermons. Until this moment I had given little credence to his warnings. Dryope was forcing a reassessment. Conflicting emotions like panicked birds filled my head.

"My heart pounded with desire to hop into the water and join her on the rock. At the same time the rational part of me urged caution for the same reason: hoping into the water.

"Now, I am not adverse to getting a little wet. There are

occasions when it is impossible to avoid, like being caught outdoors in a storm. But as a person who watches their health, I know the human body is not meant for such abuse. It is common knowledge that complete immersion in water is unhealthful, causing black bile to suffuse the liver and leading to night sweats, yellow jaundice, and in some cases even gout or worse.

My voice took on a conspiratorial tone as leaned toward Xander and said, "The truth of the dilatory effects of immersion in water was brought home to me by the plight of a man I grew up with, one Menander the Fish Monger. He claimed that the strong odors of the male body were avoidable and could be cured by regular baths and the daily putting on of clean clothes. I must admit he did smell better than I, and as a result the ladies were more apt to invite him than I to their chambers. But I believe that while the libations of water may have led to Menander having more conjugal opportunities, they lowered his resistance to disease, for the poor man developed a large pustule in his private parts, which in turn poisoned his blood leading to brain fever and death at a young age.

"So then, you can imagine my conflict. I had a very strong desire to grant Dryope's request but at the same time a fear of getting wet. So I told her, 'Why don't you come over here instead? This rock is bigger than the one you occupy. See,' I made an expansive gesture, 'Its space will allow greater scope to our hugging. And look! Yonder is a clump of grass,' I pointed. 'It looks soft, and even more comfortable, and will be handy should our activities acquire an even more amorous bent.'

"'I can't come," she answered. 'I told you this pool is my home.

It is more. It is my prison! I live here under an enchantment. I am not allowed to leave its confines. So you must come to me.' The pout was back on her lips.

"For some reason I grew cautious at this point. Did she want more than she intimated? I couldn't be sure. After all this beautiful sun dappled pool and this lovely woman were in the heart of Goblin Woods: a place of magic and danger.

"Indecision racked me for a few moments, then I decided to err on the side of caution. I would leave this grotto and this beauty and go my way.

"I knew I would regret it. I knew that visions of her would fill my nights with dreams of what might have been. Nevertheless, it was better to be safe than to be sorry.

"'I must leave now, Dryope,' I told her. 'Thank you for the drink from your pool.' Rising to leave I sincerely added, 'And thank you for a vision of beauty I will cherish a long long while.'

"'Wait,' she cried and sat up on her rock. 'Don't go away. Not yet. At least take a minute and meet my sisters before you go. They would be angry with me if I did not call them before you left.'

"How do you say no to something so pretty, so seductive? I nodded acquiescence.

"Dryope dove into the pool and disappeared. For a while the water was empty, ripples and waves crisscrossing its surface, sun light dancing on the dark and light stones that covered it bottom. Then a beautiful brown-haired girl appeared above the surface to stare at me. Like Dryope she seemed to be in her mid-thirties and at the peak of beauty and womanhood. She wore the same outfit her sister did, which is to say nothing. Soon more showed themselves around the pool. Six in all, I think. Each looking to be about the same age and as pretty as Dryope, and yet each different to. I hadn't known loveliness could take so many forms.

“Then Dryope was back on the rock. ‘These are my sisters,’ she said and proceeded to name them for me. Francesca, Geniver, and Morgana are the ones I remember. While some of the names I may forget, the memory of those bodies I'll carry to my grave and beyond. Everyone the picture of female perfection.

"’Sisters,’ Dryope said when she'd finished the introductions, ‘I called you to meet my friend before he leaves. I invited him into our pool, but for some reason he won't get in.’

"’What?’ said one, disbelief sounding in her voice.

"’No,’ said another. ‘He must join us all. The pool is wonderful. He will see.’

“At that point Dryope dove from her rock, swam over to just in front of me and standing on a boulder, rose so she was about half out of the water. Smile on her face, she reached to take my arm while her sisters gathered close around.

“I was confronted by the imploring looks of the whole bevy of them, while Dryope, one of her hands holding my biceps and the other my wrist gently tugged me towards the water.

It was as she pulled me that the back of my hand brushed the softness that was her breast. In that instant my inhibitions crumbled, my fears were set aside, and my lust flamed hot.

"I've often wondered if that contact was accidental or Dryope planned it. Regardless, it was fateful, for I found myself telling them all, 'Okay. Just let me get my clothes off and I will join you.'

"That did not take long in the state of excitement I found myself in. In a trice my garments lay in a heap and I was about to jump in when I noticed my amulet still on my wrist.

"In all my years of owning the amulet, I have taken it off only a few times and then only to hold it in my hand for some purpose. It and I have never been separated. However, if anything it liked being submerged in water even less than I do. The few times it had been dunked completely it had made a sizzling and popping sound somewhat like meat on a hot skillet. Prolonged submersion might destroy it. While I was willing to put health concerns aside, and risk night sweats to be with these exquisite females, I was not going to needlessly risk my amulet too. I took it off and laid it beside my pile of clothes.

"Ready now to join the nymphs, I went to the edge of the rock, sat down and danged my feet in the water. Dryope grabbed my arm again and at her touch any last misgivings or worries dissolved. *Night sweats be damned*, I thought, I pushed off and into the water.

"I'd sunk up to my waist when my feet encountered one of the dark boulders that covered the bottom of the pond. That stopped my decent, but only momentarily, for the rock was slippery with moss, and my feet slid into deeper water. I was about to go completely under when Dryope grabbed me and kept my head above the surface.

"She held me a moment, until I could regain my balance then let me go. Able to stand once again, I was surprised at how good the water felt. I'd expected it to be somehow distasteful, but it wasn't. I could feel the sweat that had encrusted me dissolve, while dirt and leaves that had clung to me floated away too. Maybe Menander had been right. What was a night sweat or two beside this wonderful sensation, and if that were not enough, there was Dryope too!

"You liked getting completely wet? My grandson asked. Then without waiting for an answer he said, "You won't catch actually getting down in water, not for any woman. I know better."

"So you say, but you've never had such a bevy of beauty tempting you. Anyway, she took me by the hand and led me over to her rock, then helped me up on it. 'I call my stone bed Prometheus, because of the mighty acts that take place on it,' she told me, lying on her back and gazing up to where I sat beside her.

"Looking her I thought, *This is wrong, just wrong. No woman should make me feel so helpless. I shouldn't be so befuddled by beauty.* Yet I was and despite its wrongness, I was happy about it too. I was more than happy. I was overjoyed at the prospect of what was soon to transpire between us. I wondered if she had she ensorcelled me in some manner that put me in her power? I wondered this and I didn't care. I was being carried along by a tide of lust. That she was to be mine was all that mattered. So, I leaned over to kiss her.

"The woman's beauty transformed me into something I'd never been before. I felt so strong and powerful, so much in command, that I was amazed at myself when we finished.

"As for Dryope, the experience must have been good for her too.

Her skin had a bright flush to it and she looked ten years younger. She rose, gave me another passionate kiss and then rolled off the rock and into the pool.

"*Where has she gone?* I wondered, but before I could worry about it one of her sisters crawled from the water and took Dryope's place on the rock. 'I am Geniver,' she told me. 'I am lonely too.'

"And so it went, a parade of female perfection. All wanting me. It was a dream come true. No man could ask for more beautiful or willing companions.

"After the fourth returned to the pool smiling and flushed with satisfaction and youth, I had to pause. I didn't feel as strong as I had to start with. I had some difficulty catching my breath. *But that is only to be expected,* I told myself. Regardless of the outlandish tales some men will tell you, there are limits to male endurance. *I must be approaching it,* or so I reasoned until the next sister joined me on the rock.

"'I'm Morgana, she said, and I felt my strength return at just the sight of her. As I leaned to give her a first kiss, however, I noticed that my arm looked different. The skin on it was not its usual taut self. It was wrinkled and hung loosely. *Could this be caused by the water?* I wondered. I'd heard that being wet for extended periods could cause the skin to crinkle up.

"Wondering about the rest of me, I turned to look at my reflection in the water. 'Oh, no!' I said aloud when saw it. It was me there looking back, but an old wizened version of myself. What had happened? It looked like I'd aged thirty years. I felt dizzy with shock and disbelief. Momentarily disoriented, I tumbled from the rock and into the pool.

When I opened my eyes under the water's surface I was in for an even worse shock than the one I just been dealt. The bottom of the pool was scattered with bones, and what had looked to be white stones when viewed from the above the rippled surface turned out to be arms, ribs, and bleached human skulls, their empty eye sockets staring longingly up at the warm dry air above, air that they would never again breathe or feel on skin they no longer possessed.

"Seeing the skulls I suddenly knew the fate that awaited me. The nymphs were draining me of my essence and youth. When they had all of both, they would drown me and my bones would join the others scattered around the pool's bottom.

"By the time I had put this all together Morgana was in the water with me and urging me back on to the rock. Instead, I pushed her away and headed for the pool's edge where my clothes lay.

"She grabbed me again, and I felt weak, like the old man I'd become, as I struggled in her grasp. But desperation gave me strength, and I managed to kick her hard enough she let go. I made another lunge towards the pool's edge and made it most of the way there before her arms went around me again.

"I would not give up, however, and with my last reserve of strength I dragged her to the rock where I'd left my clothes. I reached up attempting to get out of the water, but Morgana was stronger than my aged self. She was winning the battle. With a yell of desperation, I flailed my arms about trying to find something to hold on to. It was then that my hand fell on my amulet.

"Instantly there is a flash of red light that illuminated the entire pool. Time seemed to reverse for me, and I felt the years fall away, and yet elsewhere in the pool time rushed ahead at a dizzying pace. In the space of a breath or two the nymphs aged forty years, becoming gray, stooped and wrinkled old hags and crones.

"They looked at one another in revulsion, and then each gazed down at her own reflection in the pool to even greater horror. Cries of rage, despair, and desperation rang out. Morgana, released her hold on me and ducked under the surface. Others of the sisters, lead by Dryope surged across the water determined to pull me under and have their revenge.

"Free of Morgana's grasp, however, and with my youth restored, I vaulted from the pool like a seal chased by sharks. Safe again on the ledge I turned to face Dryope and her sisters.

"'Look what you have done to me,' one cried. 'I was beautiful and now I am ugly. The world was wonderful, but no more. You have taken that all away.'

"'Yes,' I told her. 'Still I find difficulty in feeling any sympathy in light of the fate you planned for me.'

"'Bah,' she answered. 'What is your life when it is hung in the balance with mine?' and so saying she swam to the far side of the pool to brood over her loss.

"Another, Geniver, tried to take a reasonable tone. Hoping to talk me into undoing things, by getting back in the pool with them. 'Death will come to you sometime, it comes to all men, and there are ways to die and ways to die. Is this not as good a time and place as any? Surely there are worse spots and ways to cross over to the other side.'

"'Possibly,' I agreed. 'But even so, death is something I wish to avoid as long as I can.'

"'Regardless, one day you must die, and graves are they not dark and lonely? Is not our pool's sunny bottom a better place?"

"And in its depths you will never lack for company,' another told me.

"'What you say has merit,' I answered her. 'I do dread the grave's moldy dankness, its cold, and most of all its lack of light. I may well return here when I feel death's bony hand on my shoulder. For the present, however...' I left the sentence unfinished.

"'Come back into the pool,' pleaded another, 'Give us back our youth, that we might entice others, jolly fellows like yourself, to join the happy band bellow.'

"'Sorry,' I told her and the sisters. 'I am about to go my way now. Don't be discouraged, however, you still have your pool and will be free to lure the next traveler to pass this way into leaving his bones upon its bottom.'

"'But you have rendered us old and ugly,' Dryope said. 'Without our beauty, without our seductive powers, how are we to accomplish that? Would you have joined us in the pool if we appeared to you looking like this?'

"'I see your point,' I said and acted as if I ruminated on their situation for a moment. Then holding a finger aloft, I offered a solution. 'I have it. You must seduce a troll into your pool's depths. The forest is full of them and they are notoriously horny, possess prodigious sexual appetites, and are not overly discriminating where human females are concerned,'

'A troll?' they cried out unison.

'Desperate times call for desperate measures,' I offered the old adage.

"'But trolls are notoriously strong. Might he not kill us instead, were we to try to pull him under?'

"I nodded, 'How very true. You must steal his youth and wear him out first, before attempting to drag him down to a watery grave. This will not be easy; trolls are famous for their sexual vigor, due it is said, to their consumption of vast quantities of river oysters. But it is only when you have completely satiated him that it will be possible to drown the creature.'

"'We must satiate him?'

"'Yes, and in the same manner you attempted to do me, of course.'

"'What?'

"'No!'

"'Never!' came the cries from around the pool.

"'Trolls, their... Their tools are said to be...' Dryope stammered, unable to voice her horrible fears.

"'I know, I know,' I commiserated. 'The price you must pay for your beauty! Still, what must be must be. Elect one of your number to go first, another second, another third, and so on. You may each have to take more than a single turn with it, but eventually the troll will become old and torpid, then you may drown it.'

"With that said I put my clothes back on and left. They were still busy arguing over which of them would first seduce a troll as their voices faded with distance.

“About a hundred yards from the pool I found the trail I had been seeking. The evening found me out of the forest, safe, and taking a good meal of stew and fresh crusty bread at the Inn of the Two Foxes.

Having finished my tale, I looked at my grandson and said, ‘And that is the story of what happened to me that day in the forest.’

“I gave him a sly look, ‘As well you may guess, I think back to that adventure often and for obvious reasons. When I do, I try to forget the nymph’s duplicity and just recall their soft warm beauty.’

“‘And now why have I told you this tale?’ I asked him.

He thought a moment and shrugged.

“‘Well, it is for this reason. I have had years to relive the adventure and have come realize that Dryope never put me under any spell of desire. It was my own greed that got me into the woods that day and my lust that got me into that pool, over to that rock, and with the nymphs. It was my own lust and greed to possess riches and beauty that drove me.’

I held up my wrist that he might again see my amulet. "If Dryope had tried to use magic on me that day to get me into the water my amulet would have turned it against her. The amulet protects me from outside forces but doesn't protect me from myself."

"This then would be my advice to you as you go off to the university. Enjoy the lovely flowers life puts in your path, drink deep of their nectar, but watch for thorns," I said.

It took him a few moments to realize that I was done talking.

Then he looked at me strangely and asked, "Is that all? Didn't you ever wonder or try to find out what happened to the nymphs?"

I sighed. He'd missed the point entirely. Wisdom is wasted on youth. They must learn for themselves. However, he looked so perplexed I told him, "No, I never returned to their pool, nor enquired after them. For I had tricked them, and I suspect they are now the playthings of whatever troll they tempted into the water. Trolls, you see, are notoriously insatiable, their sexual appetites know no bounds; nor do they age like we humans. So, try as they might the nymphs would never be able to use a troll in the manner they sought to use me. Instead the troll will have moved into their pool and uses them as often and in as many ways as he chooses. Travelers like me, lost in Goblin Woods, are now safe from the Nymphs beguilements."

My grandson took his leave of me then, and he went away at least satisfied that justice had been served. However, I fear my story taught him little of the power of languid females. Those are lessons he must learn for himself.

As for me, finding myself alone again under the cherry tree, the air warm, the breeze gentle, and sounds of my grand children at play all combined to make me drowsy once more. I closed my eyes and journeyed down a well-traveled memory, one of my favorites. A memory that took me to a pool in the forest and to women so beautiful that that even I have trouble believing that at least for a while they were mine.

The Amulet of Miraculous Reversal

Or A Grandfather's Saga

The Fifth Tale: The Princess

My first encounter with the dragon, Gwyrdd, was ten days ago. Now, many miles and a few adventures later we are about to have a second one. This one will end with one or both of us dead.

I'll admit I hold a fervent desire that it be Gwyrdd who tastes the bitter dregs of death. I want her sent on to her reward, a destination I'm confident will be one of the inner rings of hell, a place so foul that her hot sulfurous breath will be like the waft of a cool spring breeze, and where upon arrival, a horde of demons will swarm over her, clipping her wings, drawing her teeth, and declawing her, then chaining her to a rocky floor for eternity.

But wishing won't make it so, and truth be known, the odds are well in Gwyrdd's favor. Most likely I'll be the one going on to the next life. A prospect I don't relish, but at least I have hopes that no demonic crew awaits me. Instead I expect to be issued a harp and allocated a cloud top where I can strum and sing along with an angelic choir till the end of time. Not a bad fate, especially when one considers the alternative, but not a future I'm in any hurry to take up either.

But well, I am getting ahead of myself. I apologize. I pride myself on my story telling abilities, honed over years of swapping tall tales over a stoup of ale with the other elders of my village. So then, lets go back those ten days in time I mentioned.

* * *

I think I will always remember the first time Gwyrdd and my paths' crossed as The Day of the Dragon. Some might take issue with my use of the word "paths" since the dragon was flying. Be a stickler if you want, but it's my story, and that's how I tell it. So then, that day started out much like any other fall morning, however, it changed fast. I was out in front of the barn, getting the goat cart ready for a shopping trip to the village of Huddersfield. My granddaughter, Clairissa was due to arrive at our home in about a quarter hour and we were going to make that outing together.

Getting the goats into harness is no easy task as they consider cart pulling onerous and resist attachment. It was as I pulled one of the goats by a horn towards the cart that a giant shadow passed over us.
Letting go of the goat in surprise, I looked up to see a huge dark green dragon glide just over my barn's rooftop. Its wings must have measured fifty feet from tip to tip and the distance from head to tail was almost the same. I ran for what cover the barn offered. However, the dragon, ignoring me and the goats, gave a leisurely flap of its wings and cruised out over the pasture where I graze my prize-winning bull, Barzabus. The bull, a huge well-muscled creature had won many ribbons at local fairs and had brought me a small fortune in stud fees. So, it was with a sinking

heart I watched the dragon fly over Barzabus then circle to return. My fears were realized as the monster breathed fire down on the poor bull, roasting him in an instant. The hellish beast then alighted next to the smoking carcass and tearing out great mouthfuls of flesh proceeded to devour most of him.

Enraged at such foul treatment of poor Barzabus I ran for my spear and shield. I would most likely have gotten myself killed if I had actually been able to confront the beast, but had no chance, because the dragon had made short work of my bull and was just stretching out its wings prior to jumping into the air as I came back out of my house armed for combat. With over a hundred yards separating us, I could only shake my spear at the green devil as with a flap or two of its great wings, it rose over the line of trees that marked the far edge of the pasture and disappeared in the direction of our village of Pembroke.

I am glad to say that this was not a common occurrence. Dragons are rare and I had only seen one on two previous occasions, and each of those sightings was from a long distance and many years in the past. The first time I was but a youth and the second about a decade later. A good thirty years had lapsed since I last laid eyes on one. A situation I did not regret.

So, as you might guess, I was both badly shaken and seething with anger. Forgetting all about Clairissa and our trip to Huddersfield, I got both goats in harness, threw some rope in the cart and used them to drag what was left of Barzabus away to be buried.

It was only some hours later, the onerous task of disposing of my prize bull finished, that I thought of my granddaughter and our planned excursion, but I couldn't find her at our farmhouse. *Well, we'll just have to do it tomarrow*, I told myself, and so informed my wife, Tonwen.

"I hope she wasn't too disappointed when you sent her home," I said to the woman I had shared hearth and home with for over forty years. "Do you think I should send one of the farm hands to tell her we can try again tomorrow?"

"I never saw her," Tonwen informed me.

"But she was supposed to walk over from her house and meet me here."

"Well, she never showed up. Maybe she saw the dragon and stayed home. I know I would."

A cold hand gripped my heart. I had to sit down. "No," I told my wife. "It takes about forty minutes for her to walk over from her house to ours. If she was going to make it on time for our little excursion she would have been about halfway here when the Dragon came over."

"But," was all my wife could manage as she collapsed into the chair next to mine.

"I know." I said and silence hung between us for a while. Then resolution forming, I went on, "I'll saddle my horse, then follow the road between our house and hers and see if I can find Clairissa. Just pray she saw the Dragon, hid somewhere, then went the home once it was gone."

* * *

I was about half way to the home of my son, Arwel, Clairissa's father, when I found the picnic basket. My granddaughter had told me she would bring sandwiches and some drinks for us. The basket lay in the center of the road. It was crushed, but not the way you'd expect if someone struck it a blow from above or had run over it. Instead, it was smashed from the bottom up. As if it had been dropped from a great height. Seeing it I knew Clairissa was gone, and with that knowledge my life, that had been so full, abruptly seemed so empty. I felt like there was suddenly a giant hole in the center of my chest. I had to force myself to go through the motions of continuing on to her house to see if she was there. But of course, she wasn't.

Arwel was away on a business trip that had taken him to Burgundy. There was no way he could be reached without sending a messenger and that would entail a few days on horseback another week on a ship sailing for the land of the Franks and then hunting the countryside of Burgundy for him. Arwel was going to be no help in this situation. Nor was his wife, who collapsed at my news and had to have a full gill of blood drawn by our local barber-surgeon before she ceased her hysterical rantings.

On my way home, I made some plans. I would go after Clairissa. Dragons are vicious heartless killers where man and beast are concerned. This is especially true of knights. Dragons see knights as their mortal enemies and go out of their way to destroy them on sight. Where females were concerned, however, the beasts take a different attitude. Them, they carry off into slavery. Captured women are taken away to the dragon's lair where they spend their days polishing the dragon's scales, filing its teeth to fine points, neatly piling its treasure, sweeping out the beast's cave, or any other menial tasks the creature might think of.

For food the women usually are given the charred and burnt remains of the dragon's own meals. At night they sleep on the hard stone floor of the cave with no blankets and no fires to keep them warm. Hard work, poor food, and harsh living conditions meant that most of the girls the dragon brought to his lair died within a few months.

However, this meant that Clairissa was probably still alive and would remain so for a while yet. There was hope. Something to cling to. It might be only a straw, but like a drowning man I grabbed for it in desperation.

A firm resolve filled me. My life has been full of adventure. I have fought trolls, ogres, demons, fairies, witches and nymphs. They are all gone and I still live. Now I would add a dragon to my list of conquests. Or at least so I hoped.

However, in my past exploits I have been aided by a magic talisman I wear, The Amulet of Miraculous Reversal, which turns any magic directed against me back on those who would harm me. I always wear it and would continue to do so but couldn't see how it would be any help against a dragon whose size, strength, and fiery breath were physical attributes against which the amulet offered no protection.

* * *

I might be old, but when I become resolute about something, it is hard to turn me from my path. My wife, Tonwen tried to convince me to stay. "Sweet Clairissa is gone. Now must I lose you too?" she cried.

"I must try, she is our granddaughter," I told her. "But I will not go after this dragon without the means of victory. I like to think my gray hairs have brought a little wisdom with them. I will recruit our Grandson

Angwyn to join me. You know he's been studying to be a Magician for over two years now. He must know many spells and enchantments by this time. I will bring him, and he will blast the dragon by magic."

That plan, however, did not work out quite the way I envisioned. Angwyn cared a great deal for his cousin Clairissa. He wanted to help but couldn't leave home. His former housekeeper and now wife was due to deliver their first child any day. That alone had him very worried, but the midwife also had informed him the baby was breach. Angwyn spent hours consulting his books of magical instruction and lore but could find no spell to turn a baby in the womb. So, if the child did not turn on its own in the next few days, the midwife would try to turn it herself. I did not have to be told that if labor started with the baby still breach Angwyn might well loose both wife and child.

However, I could not wait the week or so Angwyn said was needed for the drama of childbirth to play itself out, and then another week to watch over the mother's recovery even if all went well. I must find another way to defeat the dragon.

"Thank you, grandson," I told him. "I must be going. Time is of the essence if I am to save Clairissa."

"But wait," he said, putting a hand on my shoulder. "I cannot go, but I can still help you some."

"How?"

"A little background here Grandfather," He told me. "As you know the Greeks were the wisest people to ever live. They taught us that all we see, touch, smell, feel, or hear is made up of four things: Earth, Air, Fire, and Water.

"As you know, magic encompasses and requires much learning and I got a late start. Most novices or apprentices start before they are ten. But I was nineteen when you helped me get my magical library and some magical adjuncts too, enabling me to begin my studies. Then too most magicians have studied under an older wiser person. I, however, have had to teach myself mostly from books. So, to make up the time and aid lost, I have confined my studies in the main to Air. It is the most common element and if I can master it, I will have achieved a great deal. So then give me a moment to think how I can put my knowledge of air to use against this dragon."

He stopped talking and paced the floor a while deep in thought before continuing, "So then dragons fly... That means they pass through air... Oh wait, I think I have it!!! Grandfather, a number of months ago I transported myself to the top of Mount Kilimanjaro, a holy place in the heart of Africa. It's peak is covered in snow year round. At its base is jungle. One thing I noticed while at its top was the absence of birds at those frosty heights. I glided down the side of the peak and eventually found birds. They were everywhere below a certain altitude but above it there were none. Back here in my study I consulted my library of magical tomes and came to realize that the air up there is too thin for them to fly. They need the thicker air for their wings to get purchase. A dragon, huge as it is, must find it doubly hard to fly in thin air."

"So," I asked.

"Just this. One of my latest achievements is a spell that may be of use to you. What if you could make it so the dragon could not fly?"

"That could be a great help. But how do I do it. I know no magic." My voice rang with despair.

"I call my spell *Angwyn's Vacuous Privation*. It thins the air in any enclosed space by about half. You'd have to catch the dragon in its cave, but there it would not be able to fly.

"I could teach you the operative syllables. Then you could work the spell."

"But I have never had the knack for memorization. Is it long?" I told him.

"Yes. That could be a problem. It is a rather lengthy and convoluted one."

"Maybe you could write them out for me. I could then read these syllables."

Angwyn stamped a foot in frustration. "I am sorry grandfather, but no, they must come, not from the eye, but from the heart to effectuate the spell."

"Then I fear this dragon will fly and fly well."

"Wait," Angwyn paced the floor again for long seconds. Then turning to me he said, "You remember our trip to the magician's fair a few years ago."

"How could I forget. It was quite an adventure."

"I still have the cockatrice we got there. I have been searching for a use to put him too. This may be it."

"What? You still have it? A cockatrice! They can be more dangerous than a dragon. At least with a dragon death is quick. I have been told that staring into the eyes of a cockatrice can cause the onset of an excruciating and cankerous condition, the body becoming covered with painful, oozing carbuncles that leave you agonizingly dead within a day."

"Yes," Angwyn said. "However, they are also magical creatures that can be taught spells. I could teach it *Angwyn's Vacuous Privation* in rather short order. You could then use it to thin the air in the dragon's den thus rendering it flightless."

My grandson then put hands on my shoulders and told me in a quite earnest fashion, "But grandfather, no matter what, you must never look into the creature's eyes. Promise me that or I can't let you use it."

"I won't. Remember it was me that first taught *you* about them. So, is he hard to take care of?" I asked.

"No, not at all, He subsists on the insects that occasionally wander into his cage. He builds traps for the crawling variety and is fast enough to pluck flies and such from the air."

"And he can cast your spell to thin the atmosphere?"

"One way to find out," Angwyn said. "Let's ask him." As we went Angwyn told me, "A cockatrice is very hard to kill. In fact the only creature known to be able to do so is a weasel, they being immune to the cockatrice's venom and stare. The best, and maybe, only way for a person to kill one is to make it see its own reflection in a mirror. Its gaze is a deadly to itself as others."

"You forget," I told him, "I was there the night you acquired the Cockatrice. I gave you these same warnings."

"I remember, it is just I want to double down on them. One can't be too careful," he said as he took me into his laboratory. There hanging in the corner of this work room was a large metal birdcage. Inside sat the cockatrice. Its head and most importantly, its eyes were covered with a hood such as falconers use to keep their birds quiet.

"Is it safe to approach?" I asked.

"So long as the cowl is in place," Angwyn told me.

I walked up to the cage and leaned over to look within. About the size of a barnyard chicken, the creature had the head and neck of a rooster, as well as the legs and feet of one too. To the back of each leg was a long fighting spur. There the similarity to a chicken ended. Its body was long and scaled resembling that of a short thick snake. The wings reminded me of a bat's, like thin black parchment stretched over a bony frame and dusted with a scattering of scales.

I was about to address the creature when it spoke first, "So Magician, I sense you bring another person to gloat over me like a monkey in a cage? When will you tire of your silly games?"

It then turned its head in my direction. "Has the magician informed that I control certain spells that can conjure him up virgins by the score and gold by the hundred weight? That in return for my freedom I will give you either or both?"

"Hold your tongue," I told the cockatrice. "Your situation has taken a dramatic turn. I am now your new master. Alas, I am too old for virgins to have much alure, and have more than ample gold. I've not come to gloat over you, but to inspect my new property and to learn what uses you might be put to. So then, from this moment on you must concern yourself with my longings and not your own. If you serve me well, I will free you, but if you do not…" I let the unfinished sentence dangle in the air a few seconds then said in a firm voice, "Well, let us just say that any disobedience on your part will result in you being dropped into a cage full of starving weasels."

"Do your worst. Death is preferable to this cage," it told me. Then the creature paused a second with its head cocked as if listening. Suddenly, in a burst of speed it was across the cage and leaping up caught a large black horsefly that had flown into the enclosure. He returned with the fly squirming in his beak. Back on its roosting bar the cockatrice stretched its head upward and swallowed the fly whole.

Fly gone, the cockatrice wiped it beak on its perch then asked, "Where were we?"

"I was telling you that cooperation will result in your freedom, but truculence will earn you a date with a weasel.

He cocked his head, "What kind of services might be expected of me."

"I want a rather complicated spell invoked at a time and place of my choosing. If you do that, I will free you."

"And if I refuse?"

"You won't. Not unless you have a death wish."

"You make it sound so easy" the cockatrice said. "Yet I smell the whiff of danger on your words. This 'time and place' of your choosing. Where and when might they be?"

"You have struck to the heart of the matter," I told the evil little beast. "I cannot tell you the exact time, yet I expect it will be within the next few weeks, as to the place, it will be in the lair of a dragon."

"Dragon! I want nothing to do with a dragon. Far better to die fighting a weasel than searing death from a dragon's fiery breath. I wish to avoid both the pain and the finality of such an ending."

"You needn't fear either pain or death. Once you have invoked the spell I will instantly free you and you can go your way while I deal with the dragon."

"How close must I get?"

"All dragons live in deep caves. You need only go just inside the entrance and there invoke *Angwyn's Vacuous Privation.* Having done so you will have completed your part of the bargain, I will free you and you may depart."

"How I long for my freedom. I have spent the last eight years in the cage of one magician or another. So, you tempt me, you tempt me."

* * *

The next day saw me up early, my horse saddled, and mule loaded with provisions, and weapons. Tied atop all rode the cage containing the cockatrice. He set up a piteous wail when he realized where he was to ride. "I am subject to motion sickness," he implored. "Swaying up here will bring it on. I do not care to spend the day in a state of nausea." I paid his complaints no mind. "Desist from eating so many flies and your stomach will not heave so."

"But the horse and mule attract a particularly succulent variety."

"Fine then, eat as many as you like. But cease your complaints." I told him as I inspected the cinch that held the load to the pack animal's back. All that remained to do was say my goodbyes to my grandson and his wife when they came out to see me off.

"Grandfather," Angwyn said when the two of them had joined me. "I have been thinking and want you to have this too," he said and held up a box shaped object wrapped in a cloth and tied with a string. It was small enough to fit comfortably in the palm of his hand.

"What is it?" I asked.

"An expansible cottage," he said. "Let me show you how it works. No spells are needed, and you can operate it yourself. First you untie the string and unwrap the cloth." He did so revealing an intricately carved thatch roofed building with windows on three sides and a door on the fourth. All was painted in detail. "Now you lay out both the string and cloth neatly in a large clear space," he said demonstrating how that was done. "Next you place the cottage atop the string and cloth. Now tap it three times with your left little finger and four times with you right thumb, thusly." When he had done that he stood back and over the course of about a minute it grew to be full size cabin.

"When it is done growing you may enter. Inside you will find comfortable sleeping quarters, as well as a table laid out each evening with fresh foods and wines. There is a library of books too. Not only will it provide for your comfort, but best of all it may save your life, protecting you from anyone or thing that might want to do you harm. As I am sure you know, the local dragons all have their lairs in the Mountain's of Dorlorn which form the Northern border of the Cloud Demon Woods. While you travel through those woods, this cottage will keep out trolls, ogres, ghosts, fairies, and any other malign influences that inhabit it. They may come tapping at the door or scratching at the windows but if you do not open to them, they are powerless to enter and harm you.

"When you are ready to travel on, just reverse the process, four raps with your thumb, three with your pinkie and it will shrink back to its original size. Tie it up again in the cloth and put it in your pocket till you next have use for it.

* * *

Ahead loomed Ys, rising from behind its tall stone walls. The city was the capitol of the small kingdom I call home.

"Why do we travel to the Ys?" the cockatrice asked from his vantage point atop the mule. I had covered the cage with a thick veil such mourning women wear. The cockatrice could see out dimly, but nobody could see in. Thus, he could determine the way of our travel, and from the tone of his voice I felt he disapproved. His next words gave truth to my surmise. "The Cloud Demon Woods, the Mountain's of Dorlorn, and the dragon's lair, none will be found within this city. I am anxious to obtain my freedom and therefore resent any side trips like this, in that they delay that glorious moment. So then, turn your horse and the mule around this instant. Let us be about our business."

"Hush," it told him. "Any more complaints and there will be no supper for you. We go to the city because, truth be told, even after you cast your spell, I will need help dealing with the dragon. So, I hope to engage the services of a dragon slayer. I've been told such a man lives here in Ys. One Herbeck the Harbinger is said to be his name. He is supposed to have killed two of the beasts.

"We are here to locate this dragon slayer. Having done so, I will entice him to join our expedition to save my granddaughter. The three of us will then proceed on to the dragon's lair where you can earn your freedom."

* * *

Now, I have always found a friendly smile and gold piece placed in the palm to loosen even the most knotted tongue. In extreme cases, a dram or two of alcohol aids in the process. However, Herbeck made no secret of the fact he stayed at the Inn of the Black Kettle, and so I found his domicile rather easily and without lightening my purse a too any great extent.

My village of Pembrook being only a day away, I am well known in Ys to be a man of means, and the innkeeper was only too glad to rent me a room, but he had reservations about allowing the cockatrice into his establishment. "That be a repugnant creature you have in that cage there," he lamented. Going on, "My other guests will not want to share the taproom with it. Can you keep it in your room?"

"I fear not. He has an enticing tongue. He may call out and tempt other guests with his wild talk of virgins and wealth. Best I keep him with me." I told the innkeeper. "Here is another coin to help you turn a deaf ear to any complaints," I said dropping a large one into his hand.

"Wellllll…" he dragged the word out until yet another coin clinked in his palm. "We can put you at a corner table in the back. It's dark there. Not many will see the cage. But what is this you say of virgins and wealth. I am not adverse to such talk myself."

"Talk is all it is. The cockatrice commands neither. But he hopes to trick the greedy and the gullible into freeing him with such illusory speech. Pay him no heed."

The cockatrice must have been listening to this exchange for he spoke now. His voice somewhat muffled by the veil hanging over his cage, "He lies. I have great powers. Would a bevy of fifty virgins satisfy you? Knock the old man down, open this cage's door, and they will be yours."

"Bah," I said. "Cockatrice, just make a single bag of gold appear here and now and I will free you myself."

"Well, it is not quite that simple," the vile little beast allowed. "It has been awhile since I conjured up any gold. I must be free to return to my home and consult certain books and tomes, refamiliarizing myself with the proper phraseology of the incantation. Then I can make it appear."

"Yes, and you are such an honorable creature, you would do so on the instant and never dream of just walking away from your obligation to give us gold," I said to the beast.

"Sir! Such an imputation wounds me."

I turned again to the innkeeper. "Tell me. How many have told you they will pay you their arrears and then done so?"

"I have become cynical of such promises and demand payment when services are rendered."

"And having become such a harsh judge of your fellow human beings," I asked him, "Are you now ready to trust this little devil?"

"Indeed not."

“Good, I will retire to my room now for a nap. Then I will return for my evening meal. At that time, I was hoping to meet one Herbeck the Harbinger who I understand resides here. Tell him that if he joins me for supper in return for his time, I will provide him with anything he likes off your menu.”

“Some of my meals come dear.”

“My purse can bear the burden.”

“That being the case, I will go and notify him of your offer now. Some of my ‘specials’ require time consuming and expensive preparations.”

*   *   *

What if he does not come to supper, or does and refuses me his help, I worried as I got ready to descend to the taproom. I had heard of no other Dragon Slayers. I wouldn’t know where to begin without this Herbeck. Showing up at the lair and rendering the dragon flightless was all very well. However, the huge green monster that had taken Clairissa away had to weigh as much as ten horses. It would not die easily or willingly. Yet, if I was to free my Granddaughter, I had to kill this beast.

It therefore followed that I simply *had* to obtain the slayer’s services. So, it was with great trepidation that went to my supper.
I worried about my clothes too. They were just my farmer’s garb. I hadn’t planned things out well, not allowing for such a contingency. Relying on Angwin’s help, I had failed to bring any of my fancy clothes with me. Still, I hoped my sincerity and my money would say more about me than what I wore. I would soon find out.

Herbeck turned out to be a huge man. Over six feet tall and well-muscled with no obvious fat. He was very broad in the shoulders and yet had a narrow waist. His hair he kept long, in a ponytail, but his face was clean-shaven. He wore leather pants and jerkin over hose and a linen shirt. His head was large, his mouth larger and when he smiled, which was often, he exposed huge horse like teeth. I took an instant liking to the fellow. When he sat down at my table, I introduced myself and we talked of this and that as the innkeeper brought tureen after tureen of food, and a seemingly endless supply of ale. Herbeck managed to consume most of this food and drink while I ate but little. Nerves had taken what little desire for feasting I might have had. I did try to keep up with him in the ale department but soon gave that up too. The man had a phenomenal appetite and appeared determined to ring every penny's worth he could out of my offer. Far from resenting this, I admired him for it.

Using a crust of bread he was mopping up the last of the juice from the bottom of what had been a platter of oysters when I slapped the table in admiration and told him, "Good for you. It gives me pleasure to see someone eat like that. There was a day I could pack it away too."

"What of me?" came a plaintive cry from the chair where I had set the cockatrice's cage. "The innkeeper maintains this establishment so well that I have yet to catch a single insect. Behold, my ribs are beginning to show."

"Here, gnaw on this," I said and dropped a bone with some meat and fat still attached into his cage.

"This is not my usual fare! Must I eat substandard food? Your whole venture depends on me, yet I am forced to starve. Oh, what I wouldn't give for one fat roach."

"What sort of hideous beast do you conceal behind that cloth?" Herbeck asked, pointing a bread crust in the cockatrice's direction.

"I will be glad to answer your question but let me tell my tale from the beginning. First, however, I think another beaker of ale is in order. It will loosen my tongue and make my storytelling all the better." "More ale, by all means," he agreed. "Those salty oysters have parched my throat."

So, it was that a serving wench came, and fortified with fresh drink I began my account of the dragon's taking of my granddaughter. The closer I came to the end of my tale and the point where I would ask for his aid, the more my elbow bent. I was so nervous about asking for his help and even more so about what his answer would be that I almost caught up with him in ale consumption.

Finally I asked. "So then, Herbeck the Harbinger, dragon slayer, can I hire you to aid me in rescuing my granddaughter. Money means nothing when weighed in the scales against Clairissa's life and happiness. You may ask any price. I will pay for your services and I will buy you any equipment you need."

"Well, I must tell you I have no desire for great riches," Herbeck said and my heart sank.

"I collected a great deal of money for the last dragon I slayed," he went on. "From it I have learned a lesson: money and me do not mix. I am too profligate in its use. I have a weakness for both wine and women, and when they are combined, I become powerless to resist. I would just squander any money you paid me in drunken wenching."

I could tell he was feeling the ale. His voice was a little slurred. His eyes did not focus well, causing him to frown or wipe them in the attempt to make them work properly. However, he spoke on, "You are a man of years. You must know stories like mine."

He held his mug up and spoke with a catch in his voice, "Just telling you of my travails with women brings my latest to mind. So then, join me in drinking to a Marie, she of the blond hair and a brief episode. For a while we danced in the sun. But now my money is gone and so is she.

"What I need isn't money, it is a song," he told me. "I need one that is of an easy tune and sad refrain. Do you know one like that?"

I shook my head. *I mustn't give up*, I told myself. *This man was necessary for the success of my mission.* To give myself a moment to think, I refilled his goblet with ale.

Being rich has taught me much about money and its uses. If he didn't want it in his pocket there might be other ways to give it to him.

"Herbeck, how about I arrange with the innkeeper to give you room and board for a year here at the Black Kettle? I could also start an account with one of the local money lenders to allow you to draw four gold pieces on the first day of every month for the next year. This would give you a place to eat and sleep and enough money to seek out life's simple pleasures, but not enough to involve yourself in excessive drinking or wenching."

He pondered this for a good thirty seconds, no doubt thinking about faded love, before he nodded his head and said, "Done." Then he stuck out a huge hand for me to shake.

I couldn't believe it. I had a dragon slayer! Between him and *Angwyn's Vacuous Privation* I began to think I might just achieve the impossible and rescue Clairissa. This called for celebration. I raised my hand and waved a serving girl over and ordered more ale.

The next hour saw us nurse our flagons while swapping tales of adventures we'd had. His favorite was my story of the time I used the Demon Raushan to defeat an ogre. I, of course, was most interested in his tales of dragon fighting. I tried not to embellish my stories too much and hoped he too did not wander too far from the truth either.

After a while we both grew silent, lost in our own thoughts. I looked around. The inn was full and the taproom seethed with the sounds of laughter, conversation, and song. Pipe smoke gathered like a fog over everything adding sweetness to the atmosphere. Life was good I told myself and would be better once Clairissa was home again.

The last table in the taproom to be filled was the one closest to ours. The innkeeper was apparently doing his best not to seat anyone too close to the cockatrice. Finally, however, all the other tables were full and he led a man in Magician garb to a seat at that table.

The man wore a black floor length tunic and a brimless pointed hat, both embellished with yellow five pointed stars and crescent moons. Tied at his waist was a sash of red silk from which hung his purse. Also, over a shoulder, he carried a pouch that, no doubt, held magical adjuncts.

His hair was dark brown, and hung to his shoulders. It framed a face that looked more used to scowling than smiling, and I couldn't decide if his large hawkish nose or piercing blue eyes should be considered his most prominent feature. Well, it made no difference, I decided and returned to my drink.

He looked us over for just a moment, then while in the act of sitting he spotted the cage resting on a chair. He must have had some magical ability to sense what was within for rising to his feet again, he asked the innkeeper, "What is this? Is your taproom now a zoo full of exotic beasts? I am not from this kingdom. Indeed I have just arrived today. I travel a great deal, so I know customs differ from place to place. Still this is an odd one. I do not think I wish to sit near such a creature. Show me to a different table."

"I am sorry sir," the innkeeper said. "This is my last table. You can take it or wait outside till someone leaves and have their seat. The choice is yours."

The magician then addressed me. "You there, farmer, the beast is yours?"

I nodded.

"Does it exude any vile odors? Must I listen to raucous outcries?"

I nodded. "For a fact its diet of insects does result in considerable flatulence. Notice the peeling paint on its cage. I lay this to the creatures gaseous exudations."

"You look to be about finished, maybe you could take it away."

"Sorry, my friend and I will be having a few more ales before we retire."

"Very well," he turned to the innkeeper, "I am tired from this day's ventures. I will take the table, but since I do so under protest you can expect no gratuity. Now, be so kind as to quickly send over a serving wench that I might order. Oh, and have her bring some red wine when she comes. I thirst."

When the serving girl returned with his order he addressed himself to it with zeal. The cockatrice chose that moment to speak to the man. "Sir," it said. "I see that you are a mighty magician, and while you may find me detestable, know that I too control powerful magics. What would you say if I offered you a hundred beautiful virgins in return for a simple service?"

"Would you shut up about virgins." I slapped the top of its cage. "Any more such talk and I will pour ale over your head." Then speaking to the magician, "I apologized for my cockatrice's interruption of your meal."

"No, no, let it speak on," the magician said. "I would hear more. For instance, creature, why do you hide behind that veil?"

"I don't. He, my master, drapes it over me. He fears my stare."

"What I fear is breaking out in carbuncles from head to foot." I told the magician.

"It can do that?"

"Yes and more. It is a dangerous creature. So then, listen to it if you like but know you will hear no truth." I told him. "The creature is the spawn of the devil, the father of lies, and this one is a liar too."

"   Still, I would hear him out."

“I have warned you,” I told him. ‘Your time is yours to waste.” I took up my flagon and took a long pull at its contents. *He may be a magician*, I thought, *but he is a fool too.*

Wasting no time the cockatrice spoke again. “This cruel man keeps me pent in this cage, hoping I will perform a service for him. Just blast him with your magic and then free me from the cage and a you will have a troupe of beautiful females at your service that are beyond the dreams of avarice.”

“What would I do with them? Many virgins would require a large household. I have nothing like that.”

“I can give you gold too, in exchange for my freedom. Enough to buy a palace to keep the women in. However, my advice would be to use them once and discard them. Such is the way of powerful men.”
“It is not the way of good men,” I addressed the magician, “And be warned, do nothing at this devil’s behest. Try no magic spells or curses on me. You will do so only to your own remorse.”

He drew himself up. “I am a wizard. I need no advice from a farmer such as yourself. I will keep my own council, thank you.”

He turned his back on Herbeck, and I and concentrated on his meal.

While eating he reached into his pouch and took out a small notebook, which he consulted between bites of food and sips of wine. I worried he was studying some spell. I worried that my warnings had fallen on deaf ears. I worried that what had started out as a wonderful evening might end in strife.

I thought any difficulties would wait till he had finished his meal. I was wrong. My worries came true before he had consumed half of it. He paused in his eating and turning in his chair ask me, "Old man farmer, you don't have a weak heart do you?"

I shook my head.

"Good. And have you ever heard of the spell known as *Galvics' Voltaic Rousing*? It can prove intensely stimulating, especially if delivered at its most potent level, such as I propose for your experience." So saying, he reached into his tunic and pulled out a wand that he pointed at me while speaking some strange syllables. As he did so the ruby like red stone in my Amulet of Miraculous Reversal began to glow. When a beam of greenish light came from his wand it only made it half way to me before being met by a red one from my amulet. The two beams then blended into a glowing red vortex that dripped great drops of greenish light which fell to the floor. This went on for a moment or two then the green beam ceased, and the red finished crossing the gap between us and engulfed the magician.

He managed a, "What?" before being enveloped, and then letting out startled cry of anguish he leaped high into the air. He crashed down on his back to lay there shuddering, jerking, and bellowing as hundreds of tiny lightning like sparks about a half foot long danced over his body singeing his hair, clothes, and any exposed skin. The small volume he had been consulting was also reduced to ashes as was his pouch of magical adjuncts. After about a half minute, but only when his roarings and twitchings stopped, did the voltaic rousings also cease.

"   Now see what you have done?" I shouted at the cockatrice. "Maybe this will cool your lies," I told it as I poured the rest of what was in the ale beaker over the creature's head.

This elicited a howl from the beast. "Injustice! Injustice!" It raged. "Why must I always suffer such?"

Paying no heed to its rantings, I turned to Herbeck and said, "I think you'd best fetch the innkeeper."

"No need, I see him coming now."

It was true. Having heard the magician's outcries and seen the startled reactions of those at tables around us he was hurrying over. When he got there, I explained what had happened. He had heard of my Amulet of Miraculous Reversal and understood immediately.

"Here is what I think," I told him. "This magician will be out cold for at least a few hours. However, when he wakes, I fear he will be in a vengeful mood. Magicians in such a frame of mind can be dangerous. He may foolishly seek to settle any scores he holds against your establishment or more likely, my person. I recommend that you send for the King's Watch and have this fellow put in the Null Chamber. It is room located deep in the King's dungeons that obviates any and all magics, spells, or enchantments performed from inside it. It was made by a powerful sorcerer for just such occasions. A few days in there and hopefully he will see the error of his ways and reform. If not the king has wizards in his employ that can transfer this fellow to a far land, or possibly another planet. If such threats don't calm him, they can even strip him of his powers if needs be."

The innkeeper nodded. "Yes, I know of and have had occasion to use the King's Null Chamber. In those instances, it was drunken magicians I consigned to its darkness. This will be the first malicious one. Still, it seems the perfect place for this fellow to spend his next few days." So saying, the innkeeper went of the fetch the watch.

I turned to Herbeck, "I have had enough for a night. I have drunk too much and thanks to my cockatrice I have a new enemy. But I also have a new friend," I told him as I put a hand on his shoulder. "I am off to bed, and after the amount of ale I have consumed I will not want to rise early. Can we meet in the stables at noon and make our departure for the Mountains of Dorlorn."

Herbeck nodded. "I will gather all I need to kill this dragon and meet you then."

* * *

Evening was fast approaching and we had just passed by a comfortable looking inn when Herbeck asked me if we were going to camp out for the night.

"If so, I know of a nice spring that fills a lovely pond not far from here."

Silently thanking Angwyn for his generosity I told Herbeck, "Camping is not part of my plan," I told him. "Let's keep going a while longer. Show me were this pond lies, then I have a surprise for you." There was a surprise in store for me too for when I unwrapped the tiny expansible cottage. I found it had changed and now had a barn like attachment on one side and some sort of addition on the other side. I am always careful about magic and not understanding these new appendages to the miniature cottage I wondered if I should even do the tapping routine that made it grow. But then, my grandson would not give me anything dangerous, or so I told myself, and tapped away.

When it had grown to full size I was pleased to see that it had expanded not only in size but had anticipated our needs for the night. The barn-like addition was a stable full of hay and oats for our horses and mule. The second new addition to the cabin was a second bedroom for Herbeck's use.

The food laid out looked and smelled exceptionally good. I love freshly baked bread and there was a loaf, the aroma of which tempted me to forget my manners and start eating without Herbeck. However, I restrained myself.

I found that even the Cockatrice was allowed for. On a side board, well away from our food I found a plate containing a number of roaches lying on their backs and laid out for his evening repast.
"Well now," he could hardly contain his excitement when I put the plate in his cage. It snapped up one of the insects and with its mouth full, managed to mumbled, "It is about time. This is the best tasting meal I have had in days."

I had yet to eat myself and the cockatrice's grunting pleasure while crunching and smacking were going to spoil my appetite so I picked up his cage and put it in the bedroom I would use and closed the door on his feasting. Normally this would have elicited a howl of indignation from the creature, but the foul little thing was too busy eating to notice.

Herbeck was still getting the animals fed and settled in for the night, so I started a fire in the fireplace, lit the lamps, and carrying one with me went to look over the library.

I found a number of books that might interest me and I was trying to decide which to read when Herbeck came in.

Walking over, he looked down at the table heaped with food. "Now that is a sight worth waiting a hungry afternoon for."

"Agreed," I said and we both took up our plates.

Herbeck was still packing it away when I gave up and retreated to an easy chair. I set my half-drunk beaker of wine on a side table and reached into my jacket for my pipe and tobacco. Soon I was puffing away and a sweet-smelling gray cloud was filling the room around me.

Having enjoyed that bowl, knocked the dottle out, and was refilling when the dragon slayer took the other easy chair.

" So then," he started the conversation. "You are a rich man. You want for very little in this life. Tell me of this girl that you will risk loosing such a life for."

I described her for him. A pretty girl, just turned eighteen, tall and thin with auburn hair, and smiling eyes and mouth.

"I've killed two dragons," he told me. "The first because I was attacked by it. It was just self-defense. The second however, because I was hired to go after it. Another man like you, this time with a daughter taken, heard that I had slain one and offered me payment to kill the one that had captured his girl, and to bring her back to him. He was generous with his money and paid me well when I succeeded. But he never risked his own life in the adventure, just his money."

Herbeck took a drink from his goblet before going on, "You are richer still. They say you have more money than the king. Yet here you are putting your life at risk. How is that?"

" I do not know the reason," I told him. "Blood. Kin. Love. They all are motivations. Oh, and a thrust for revenge. Did I not tell you? The dragon killed and ate my prize bull, Barzabus."

Herbeck laughed. "Oh yes, your prize bull. Well, that explains all."

I pondered a moment. "I had a blessing once, given me by a king. I was told I would have wonderful grandchildren. That describes Clairissa. Wonderful. I guess if you knew her you would understand better. She has always been a favorite of mine.

"I call her The Princess. When Clairissa was a child and she and her cousins would get together to play, and when it was her turn to pick the game, she never wanted to play "house." Clairissa wanted to play "Castle" or sometimes "Royal Marriages." She would be the Princess and her cousins the ladies in waiting. She would make up elaborate schemes with the boys invited to be knights and fight to save both hers and their girl cousins' virtue. In these games the poor village cats and dogs were seen as ogres and trolls for the boys to chase off.

"As she grew older such games no longer of interested her, yet she still wanted to be a princess. Her parents could not afford to buy her the fancy clothes she wanted so she taught herself stitchery. She worked hard to make money and saved it up to buy fancy pieces of cloth, then inveighed on me to take her to Ys where she could see what the latest styles being worn by fancy ladies were. Once she's seen the latest fashions, it was home again and working from drawings she had made she sewed up similar items for herself.

"Someday I will met a prince," she told me once, while she pirouetted in a new outfit she'd made. "If he is to notice me, I must look like a fine lady."

"A beauty like you, he would notice if you wore rags." I told her.

"Oh, Grandfather, you just say that because you love me," and I had earned a hug.

" And she is right, Herbeck, I love her. I can't leave her to that dragon. And I can't just leave it up to you either. I have to be there. To see the creature die. Maybe even weld the death blow. Who knows how many families that beast has destroyed, how many men has it killed, how many girls taken into slavery? It has to be stopped."

" Which brings up an interesting question" Herbeck said. "Which dragon are we after. There are five that live in the Mountians of Dorlorn. We need to identify which one took Clairissa or we may have to kill them all to find her."

"I got a good look at it. It flew right over me not a hundred feet in the air. But he just looked like a green dragon to me. Nothing special. No distinguishing marks."

"Well," Herbeck said. "Green ugh? That can only be Gwyrdd. The others are two blacks, a yellow and a white. Oh, and you said, 'He,' but it is a she. As I mentioned her name is Gwyrdd and she's crazy mean. She has the foulest temper of the lot. Doing away with her will be doing this whole island a favor."

"Gwyrdd? A strange name and hard to say," I said.

"Oh, not so odd," the dragon slayer said, waving his cup about. "It's said she was born in Wales, and I believe her name is Welsh for green."

"That explains it. Welsh! Have you ever heard someone speaking Welsh?"

"Can't say as I have."

"Most of their words start out sounding like the gagging noise a dog makes when it is about to throw up."

" A vomiting dog? Yes. 'Gwyrdd' does sound that way." He laughed and toasted me with his cup before draining it.

"Now I have a question for you," I told Herbeck. "I saw most of what you brought as we unloaded our pack animals. You have no armor, just a shield. No spear. You might have something sharp, a sword or the like wrapped in that leather bundle of yours. I did see a powerful stave. Still I have to wonder how you propose to kill this Gwyrdd."

" Fighting a dragon one needs to be agile. That is why I have no armor. It would slow me down. The bundle you saw contains arrows. Heavy iron tipped arrows. And what you thought a stave is in fact my bow. It is English. Made of Yew."

At this point in his narrative Herbeck got up and retrieved his bow and strung it. Holding it out to me he said, "Here, try to pull it."

I did and trying as hard as I could didn't draw it back more than a few inches. He then took it from me and holding its center in his left hand, pulled. The muscles in his great shoulders bulged under the strain but the string came back till he held it next to his cheek. He then released the string and it made a powerful twang.

"Don't feel bad. Not many men can draw my bow. You must be taught from your youth, pulling progressively stronger and stronger bows as you build your strength over the years. Only then can you use such a bow. With it I can sink an arrow four inches deep in a pine tree." He said while unstringing his bow and retaking his seat.

I was almost ecstatic as I refilled his cup. "This Gwyrdd does not have a chance against such a weapon. Clairissa will be home in a week."

"I hope it is so," he said. "But a dragon's scales are harder than iron. Harder than Roman Centurion's armor. More arrows, even such as mine, will bounce off than pierce her hide. I must hit her squarely and in a critical spot. Even then a bit of luck will do no harm.

"In spite of having a bow such as mine, the advantage should still lie with the dragon. I think, however, this magic of yours to render her flightless will tip the scales in our favor.

We talked of many things after that, he mostly of women. His stories were good, but not nearly as good as my adventure with the water nymphs. I was tempted to tell him that tale, but by then the fire had grown low, and the wine had made me sleepy. I took my leave of him and went to my room. The bed was exquisitely soft and smelled of flowers. The wine had made me more tired than I thought. Even the cockatrice's rants against being left in a dark room all evening did not keep me awake.

* * *

Having the expansible cottage to protect us at night, we decided to take the shorter direct route to the Mountains of Dorlorn. We could have gone around Goblin Woods and approached them from the north, but cutting through the woods would save us about three days travel in getting to Gwyrdd's lair.

Worried as I was about Clairissa, I thought those three days saved would be worth any added danger to ourselves.

* * *

Our first night in Goblin Woods convinced me that I would have to speak to Angwyn about his expansible cottage when I returned home. He was going to have to do something about sound proofing it. I got very little sleep that night.

Almost as soon as it got dark outside, a ghost found us. At first it just went around and around the cottage time and again, as if it might find something new each time. I could hear it dragging its chains which must have been heavy for when they clanked it was a deep cumbersome sound. After maybe an hour of circling, it tried rattling the windows and pounding on the door.

This set the cockatrice to alternately yelling at it to go away or asking it to break in and free him. In desperation, I threw a blanket over the evil little beast's cage in hopes of shutting him up, but it had the opposite effect, instead enraging the creature and setting him to pronouncing all sorts of curses on Herbeck and I.

I shook the cage. "I will remove the blanket only if you allow me to put your hood on and you cease making any sounds. The ghost is bad enough without you adding to the cacophony. So then, will you cease your noise?"

"But I wish to communicate with this creature," the devilkin said. "We may discover we have mutual acquaintances. Then too, it is possible death has not robbed him of all desire for female companionship. I could offer him my services?"

" The ghost will not free you. I will free you, and I will do so only when you cast *Angwyn's Vacuous Privation* over the dragon Gwyrdd's lair. So then, you will cease all noise, or I will leave the blanket in place and put you and your cage in the stable with the animals. Which is it to be?"

" Oh very well," he agreed then in a sour grapes tone went on, "As a rule, ghosts are only interested in souls to feed on anyway. I will hold my tongue."

I nodded and pulled away the covering. I had barely refolded the blanket and placed it back in the cupboard when the ghost took to wailing. Having failed in all its efforts to find a way in it set up high pitched piteous cry that evoked feelings of loneliness, sorrow, and faded love. They almost made me feel sorry for the creature except I knew that if it once got among us we would all die horrible deaths.

* * *

The next two nights were for the most part peaceful. Creatures of one kind or another might come by and try to gain entry, but having failed they moved on and left us alone. I could sleep.

The Mountains of Dorlorn were getting near. Each time the trees thinned enough that we could see the horizon to the north the jagged peaks seemed closer as they spread across our view like the jagged teeth of a basilisk.

When the ground started to slope upward I knew we were getting close. Then the trees changed, oak and hardwoods replaced by pines and juniper. For the most part the trees still grew thick, giving us good cover, but there were times when the space between trees opened so we could be seen easily by Gwyrdd if she should fly over us. Herbeck took to carrying his bow slung over one shoulder and his quiver over the other. We both had our eyes on the sky most of the time, and let our horses pick their own way over the ground.

We had gone on this way a good while when my horse began to nicker. Looking around to see what had disturbed the animal I saw sunlight glinting off something metallic in deep grass nearby. Riding over I found a knight sprawled out on the ground under some nearby trees. He lay unmoving and in full armor. Not far away a huge horse almost double the size of ours, and also armored, was lazily cropping some grass.

"Herbeck, look," I pointed as I hopped down from my saddle. "I wonder if he is alive?"

"	Don't go too close," Herbeck said while nocking an arrow and drawing the bow.

I immediately saw the wisdom of his advice. This *was* the Goblin Woods. Rarely would anyone or thing met here be friendly. So, I found dead branch under one of the trees and standing well back, lightly prodded the fellow. Nothing.

I did it again, this time with a little more force. Still no movement, but I did hear a low moan from the man.

“ I think he is injured,” I told Herbeck.

“Use your branch to open his visor if you can.”

“Good idea,” I agreed and still keeping well back, used the limb to lever it open.

He *was* injured; his face a mask of blood. “He’s going to need our help,” I told the dragon slayer. “Come down here and assist me.” Together we managed to get his helmet off. He had a large swelling on his forehead. It was lacerated too, and the cut was the source of the copious bleeding that had run down over his face.

I pried up an eyelid. The pupil got smaller as it was exposed to the light. That was a good sign, or so I had been told somewhere and time.

“I am no barber/surgeon,” I told Herbeck. “But I think he just needs some rest. I know we were going to ride on for another hour. Still, we should set up the cottage here and get him into a bed. He can have mine.”

“ What?” exclaimed the cockatrice. It must have been listening to our conversation. “Know you not that knights draw dragons like bull droppings draw flies. Leave him where he lays and let’s be as far as we can from here by nightfall.”

I stared at the cockatrice a few moments then told Herbeck, “I might be tempted to agree with the evil little beast. However, Angwyn told me the cottage was proof against whatever we might meet in the forest. That includes dragons.” I turned to the cockatrice again, “Have you already forgotten what happened two nights ago when that troll that tried to break in but accomplished nothing, not so much as loosening the door in its frame. It does not even show scratches. Trolls are remarkably strong, and yet that one could do nothing." Speaking again to Herbeck I said, "So what do you say, let's set the cottage there, under those trees, and see how this knight fellow is in the morning? Besides my neck is sore from staring at the sky all day. A little liquid refreshment might ease the tight muscles."

It was as if the gods approved of my actions too, for when I unwrapped the small cottage there was another room adjoining the side of the building just as had happened when Herbeck joined me. When the cottage was set up and expanded we found not only larger portions of food, a third bedroom, and an extra stall in the stable.

The two of us dragged the knight into the new sleeping area, stripped off his armor and the padding he wore under it and laid him out on the bed. As I was leaving the room I noticed that a basin of warm water and bandages had been laid out on a side table. The cottage was again anticipating our needs. Taking this as my cue, I cleaned the dried blood from his face and hair and wrapped his head in bandages. That done, it was time for a drink. I went back out into the main room to find that Herbeck already had one poured and waiting for me.

* * *

I t was in the wee hours of the morning that I heard moans coming from the knight's room. I got up, trimmed my lamp's wick for a brighter flame and went to see how our wounded guest was faring.

He was tossing and turning.

I set the lamp on the bed stand, pulled up a chair to sit in, and touched him lightly on the shoulder. “How are you feeling?” I asked. He opened his eyes and looked around. There was not much to see. The lamp only threw a little light.

“Who are you? Where am I?” He inquired.

“A friend and I found you lying under a tree. You’d been hurt. We brought you to this cottage in hopes you might get better. What is your name?”

He hesitated a moment before saying “I am Sir Bravus, a knight of Melekhan.

“How were you hurt?” I asked.

“I am not sure,” Sir Bravus said. “I was chasing after the dragon Gwyrdd. I was riding hard and passed under a tree. Something hit me hard. I ran into a low hanging branch I suspect.”

“ That would explain the blow to your head,” I told him.

He reached up and gingerly fingered the bandages I had swathed his head in.

“Something gave you a good whack. Under those wrappings you will find a large swelling and a sizable cut that will no doubt leave a fine scar for the ladies to admire.”

“Did you fix me up”

“Yes. I have, through necessity learned a bit of the medicinal arts.”

“Thank you. Now I must get up.”

He made to rise from the bed, but I pushed him back down.

“Morning will be soon enough for that. You need to rest.”

"But I am awake now," he protested.

"No, after such an injury you need to rest. If you cannot sleep, tell me, for it may be some black bile has gotten into your blood. If so, I will need to bleed you."

"No, no!" he sounded a little fearful. "I can sleep."

"Good," I said, not surprised that he was frightened. I have known many men who will face battle bravely, but fear a barber/surgeon. This is a fact I am not above taking advantage of, nor was this first time I used such anxiety to get my way with a warrior. So then, I told him, "I will leave you now, go back to sleep and we will get you up and out of bed in the morning."

I returned to my room, taking the lamp with me. His room was left in total darkness again, and I felt confident that he wouldn't rise until the morning sun lightened the chamber.

I was correct. The sun was just pinking the horizon when I heard him moving about and so got up myself. I had not been up this early any morning while staying in the expansible cottage and was in for a treat as I walked out into the living area. As I looked around I saw the sideboard where we got our food shimmer a few moments then solidify again, but this time covered with the makings of our morning meal.

Suddenly my nose was in paradise as the smells of bacon, fried sausage, potatoes, and eggs, as well as other wonderful odors filled it. My mouth watered and my stomach hungered in anticipation of the treats that would soon fill it.

Sir Bravus came out of the chamber where he had slept to find me looking over the feast laid out for us. He appeared to be following his nose and then said, "You did not tell me your name last night, but you must be a gentleman to set such a fine table."

"   Yes, well I wish I could take credit for it. However, the food and this lovely cottage are the result of a spell worked by my grandson, Angwyn. He is a budding magician."

Hearing us talk, I guess, had awakened Herbeck, for yawning and stretching he chose that moment to join us. He too had eyes only for the food laid out before us. I, however, remembering my manners introduced the two. "Herbeck, I want you to meet Sir Bravus, a knight of the Kingdom of Melekhan, Sir Bravus, this is Herbeck the Harbinger, a dragon slayer of great renown. Herbeck, you may be interested to know that this gentleman's injuries came as a result of chasing Gwyrdd. So, we three have a common detestation of that particular dragon."

Without further formalities, the three of us laid into the feast set out for us. I had just set a plate heaping with the cottage's bounty on the table and was pulling up my chair when I heard a plaintive cry from my bed chamber, "What of I? Am I to be left to starve? Lo, I may count my ribs. See how I waste away. Is nothing laid out for me?"

"Who is that? Inquired Sir Bravus. "Is there another person staying here? Or is that your wait staff I hear."

"No, it is a wicked cockatrice I keep caged. To explain his presence would be to jump into the middle of my story. Let it unfold from the beginning and you will understand," I said as I pushed my chair back and rose. I looked where the cockatrice's platter of roaches had previously been found. This morning a plate of shiny black beetles were laid out for him and he seemed delighted when I gave them to him, saying, “Ahhh. Stink Bugs. How luscious.” He then pecked one into his mouth before going on, “I will be sad when you free me and I must catch my own meals. This cottage spoils me.”

I went back to my own meal, my hunger somewhat dampened. “Herbeck, at this evening’s meal, I think it will be your turn to feed that vile creature. I am going to loose weight if I continue to do so. One need only watch him eat to loose almost all desire for food.” So saying I took a tentative bite of breakfast. I have to confess that my taste buds delighted so in the food that my appetite returned and my plate was practically clean when I pushed back from the table.

While we ate I told Sir Bravus my story and how Herbeck and I happened to be approaching Gwyrdd’s lair when we had found him. Meal over, we all went to softer chairs set out for our use. When we were seated I asked the knight if he would relate his own tale of how he also came to be here in Goblin Woods and near the dragon’s lair.

“I am Sir Bravus a Knight of the Kingdom of Melekhan,” he told us. Again I thought to detect some hesitation on his part. Not that I thought he lied, but there was more he was not saying. This I felt sure of. However, wanting to hear further of his tale, I did not press him for more about who he was.

“The dragon Gwyrdd has been ravaging our kingdom for years. Our knights are defeated. Our maidens carried off. Our villages burned. Our cattle and pigs eaten. The whole kingdom is impoverished by her depravations. One day I heard our King plead, “Who will rid me of the turbulent beast?”

"Hearing his words, I knew it was my calling. Just as some knights know that they are destined to go on a quest for the Holy Grail, so I knew it was my fate to search out and kill Gwyrdd, and that is what I am about.

Bravus, to agitated to stay in his chair and got up to pace the room. "Towards evening, day before yesterday, as I rode through the woods below Gwyrdd's lair I heard the voices of some men crying out for help. Following the sound, I carefully approached a clearing in the woods. There I found six men with their feet chained to stakes. The stakes formed a large circle around a huge egg that sat on a small hump. I knew instantly what was happening. The egg had to be that of a dragon. Nothing else lays anything so large. Due to its proximity to Gwyrdd's lair, it must be hers. The men were staked out to provide fresh food for the hatchling dragon when it emerged.

"Coming out of the trees I spoke to the men. 'Who are you?' I asked. I got a number of answers and concluded they had been collected from various towns and villages that surround Goblin Woods. Having identified themselves they immediately began asking for food and their freedom. Using my horse I pulled each of the stakes from the ground. As I did so I kept asking them more and more questions and their plight emerged.

"They had been collected about four days previously. Each had been carried to this location and chained to one of the stakes. One man was close enough to a stream that ran through the meadow that he could dip various pieces of clothing the others passed to him in the water and then pass it back to the owner. They then could suck the water from the cloth and slake their thirst. However, they'd had no food since their captures, and all were ravenous by the time I found them.

"After being left alone, tied to their stakes for two days, the dragon returned and laid an egg on the grassy hump in the center of their circle, leaving them like flower petals spread around it. Its egg laid, the dragon left, and they'd spent two more days crying for help and getting hungrier and hungrier until I came along.

"I did not have enough food to share with them, but then an idea occurred to me and I had the men collect fallen branches and twigs from the surrounding woods. When we had enough for a goodly fire, I piled kindling and the larger branches around the egg. Then I lit a fire. I can't sure, due to the loud crackling of the wood as it burnt, but as the fire reached it peak, I thought I heard some plaintive squeaking from the egg."

Sir Bravus stopped his pacing and with a smile told us, "After about twenty minutes the fire died down and I brushed the ashes aside. Fetching my mace it was but the work of one or two heavy blows to crack the egg open and let the dead dragon flop out onto the ground. "If you are hungry," I told them, "Here is meat enough to fill all your bellies."

"Needing no further encouragement, they fell on the dragonet tooth and claw. In just minutes the young dragon was reduced to a scattering of viscera and blood stained bones.

"I knew that the dragon's wrath would be kindled when she realized the fate she had planned for the six men had instead befallen her young one. I interrupted their contented sighs and burps, telling them, 'You must leave here as soon as possible.'"

"Having said that I retrieved the jaw bone from the scattered refuge that had once been the dragonet. Using a knife pried out a tooth for each of them. 'Keep these with you till you get out of Goblin Woods. The creatures that the call the woods home will sense the teeth and leave you alone. But you must go now and go quickly. They will be of no protection should the dragon find you. They will only infuriate her, and literally enflame her wrath.'"

"Within minutes they were all gone. I, however was not going to leave. This might be my chance to kill Gwyrdd. When she discovered the fate of her dragonet, and her heart filled with rage and sorrow, she might be distracted enough that could take her unawares and slay her.
"So the next little while saw me collecting branches and building a blind under one of the trees. I was careful in selecting a site down wind of spot where the egg had lain so she would not catch my scent. I was also careful in the construction so that the branches at the front gave me adequate cover but would fall aside in an instant and let me spring forth on my charger should the opportunity for a sally present itself.

"Once hidden I waited. There was no guarantee she would come, but the men had said she had been away for two days. It seemed logical she might come to check on the egg.

"The afternoon was well along when I heard, 'I am coming. How are you my darling?' as if from a great ways off." It was Gwyrdd." Bravus paused in his tale and looking at us said, "You are aware that a Dragon's mouth, with their stiff lips and forked tongues do not lend themselves to human speech. The only sounds they can make are roars and screeches. However, dragons have perfected the art of projecting their thoughts. Humans, other dragons, or any sentient creature for miles around can 'hear' the dragon's thoughts. It is as though they spoke, and you heard them, but by some magic no real sound is involved."

Herbeck nodded his head in sage agreement, however, I had never heard such a thing. Bravus assured me it was so before going on with his story. "She flew low over the egg mound. 'Have you already hatched? I see your egg is open and a scattering of bones. You have eaten well. Shall I fetch you some more men in the morning?'

"She flew off, circled and flew back. 'Why do you not answer me, my little one? Where are you?'

"Having said that she landed next to the egg mound and studied the collection of bones, egg shell, and ashes. It was not long before she said, 'O perfidy! My poor hatchling. My little dragonette. O treachery! How could such a thing have happened? Eaten by man creatures! Never will you soar through the sky. Never will you breath fire down on your enemies.' She was silent for awhile then throwing back her head she let out roar of rage and sorrow while at the same time projecting as loud as she could, "Hear me men who killed my little one. I will hunt you down. I will kill you, and I will eat you."

"I watched all this from my blind. Regretably she had landed facing me and I could not charge. She would see me coming and swat me like a fly. So I stayed in hiding.

"She only spent a few moments in mourning then seething with rage she gave a great flap of her wings and was airborne. She must have seen footprints or some indication of the direction most of the six men I had freed had fled in. At any rate she was off and, on their trail, flying close to the ground so she could hunt them.

"When she was gone, I came out of the blind and took off after them too. I could not just abandon those men I had rescued to their fates. I set a quick pace hoping to catch up. Alas, I was to be of no help. Riding under a tree, I must have hit my head on a low branch that knocked me out left me for you to find."

Having said all that, he got up to pace the room. However, after a turn up and down he had to lean on a chair for support. "Dizzy," he said.

"Not unusual, that dizziness," I told him. "Not after a blow to the head such as you've had."

"I must overcome it," he stated. "I wish to join you two in killing the beast. However, I must not be a burden, but instead an asset."

I smiled at him. "I welcome you. The more the merrier. A skilled knight mounted on a magnificent destrier such as yours could only increase our odds of success. So, we would love to have you join us. If you can just ride your horse for now, that should be enough. We have planned to sneak close to her lair today. Then we will strike early tomorrow. That gives you a full day to get back into fighting trim. Do you think it will be enough?"

"I am sure it will."

* * *

We packed up and were soon on our way again. Finding a game trail that went in the direction we wished to go, we followed it. The way grew steep, but now a thick pine forest covered the mountain side giving us good cover. About noon, Herbeck called a halt. "We must be very close now," he told us. "I will go on ahead on foot and scout out the location of Gwyrdd's lair."

This did not suit me. I wanted to go along, but Herbeck insisted he go alone. He being the dragon slayer I acquiesced. I was not happy, however. Stuck there, sitting on a rock under a tree, visions of Clairissa in the dragon's cave haunted me. It might have been my mind playing tricks on me, but I felt I could sense the dragon, feel it close by, hear a rumble deep in its chest and catch a whiff of its sulfurous breath on the wind.

I knew such thoughts to be ridiculous. Then, however, I realized I might be feeling just what my granddaughter was experiencing at that very moment. We had always been close, could almost read each other's minds. Was I sensing what she was sensing? If so, then maybe she would know what I was thinking. So I told her, "I'm coming. Be brave and tomorrow we will be together again."

Sometime later, when Herbeck had been gone about an hour I saw Gwyrdd. Just momentarily, only a glimpse, seen between the trees as she soared high overhead in the direction of Goblin Woods. *Some poor creature that calls the forest home will not see the coming night,* I told myself then kinda sorta prayed. Not something I do very often, but his time I said: *Let it be a troll or an ogre, something that richly deserves its fate, not some innocent person or halfling the beast finds. Oh, and whoever, or whatever they are, let them be the dragon's last meal. Ever!* Having seen the beast, I could sit no long and rose to pace back and forth.

"Where's Herbeck," I demanded of Bravus.

That only got me a raising and lowering of the shoulders from the knight who could no more know where the dragon slayer had gotten to than I.

Another half hour pacing and worrying saw me just on the point of ignoring Herbeck's instructions to stay with the knight and the pack animals and go looking for him. I was about to tell Bravus what I was going to do, when Herbeck returned.

Just seeing him, such a burden was lifted from my shoulders. When he smiled, showing those big horse like teeth of his, I knew all was well.

"Found the lair," he announced.

I didn't need to hear that. His smile had already told me. What I needed were details that a grin could not convey. "So… So…" I said making a *give me* gesture at the same time.

"It is about a mile from here. Maybe a thousand feet higher up the mountainside. This mountain is honeycombed with caves and at first, I despaired of finding which she calls home. Then I saw one with a huge midden below its opening. Gwyrdd has been tossing out bones and debris for centuries. It has made quite a pile below the entry. Oh, and that entrance is huge. But then it'd have to be for her to fly in and out, wouldn't it? I guess it is a good hundred feet across and in an arch shape, flat on the bottom and with semicircle above.

"I couldn't see much detail of what's inside. Too dark. I can say that at least the first few feet are flat rock with a few large boulders here and there. After that, well, we will find out tomorrow."

"All you will find out is what the inside of the dragon's gullet looks like. It will be the last thing you ever see," said the cockatrice from its cage tied atop the pack horse.

"Hush you little devil," I told it, "Or you will get no supper."

"On the contrary," it said. "We are in striking range of the dragon's lair. It is too late to turn back and your whole strategy hinges on my casting the spell *Angwyn's Vacuous Privation.* Without me you will fail. So then, here are my demands: First, I want some respect from you all. You will address me as 'Sir' while giving me a slight bow. Second, I want this veil off my cage, I can hardly see through the mesh. Besides that, it keeps insects out. Third, I will…"

" Herbeck," I interrupted the vile creature, "Would you be so kind as to get me that box with the holes in it that I keep tied to the rear of this pack horse's load."

" Do not ignor me," the cockatrice screeched. "I am telling you what I require for my continued cooperation in this fool hardy adventure. So take heed."

"No, you take heed. When I acquired you, I told you that you that if you did as I command you would earn your freedom. Anything else and I would turn a staving weasel loose in your cage."

Having said that I turned to Herbeck and the box he had fetched. I opened it and reaching inside withdrew a good sized weasel. Then using my other hand reached in again and pulled out a second.

They were rather placid in my grasp until I held them close to the cockatrice's cage. When I did that they squirmed and twisted in anticipation of a good meal.

The cockatrice, seeing the weasels, let out a horrified squawk then jumped down from its perch and fled to the corner of it cage farthest from the hatch. “No, no,” it implored. “Feed me not to weasels. Their claws are sharp and their teeth will tear my flesh.”

“So then,” I asked the cockatrice, “Who is going to experience what’s alimentary canal in the near future? Is it I in Gwyrrd’s gullet or you in these weasel’s?”

“Mercy, Master, Mercy,” the cockatrice implored. “I fear being rendered and torn apart by weasels and I fear the death that will result from such abuse.”

“So then, you call me ‘Master,’ again?” I asked the cockatrice.

“Yes Master. Mercy, Master.”

“And we will hear no more of ‘Demands’ from you?”

“An innocent slip of the tongue, Master. I meant to say ‘Requests,’ just ‘Requests.’ I only wanted to ask if you would be kind enough to procure me some tangy mustard sauce to put on tonight’s beetles. That is all. No Demands. Now please, put those weasels away. They are an impediment to our friendship.”

* * *

Herbeck had also found a cave where we could set up the expansible cottage and it would be out of sight. We did so and then settled in for what might be our last night. As we sat down to dinner it was with the knowledge that the morning would see us attempting to kill Gwyrdd in her lair. Bravus and Herbeck both ate big meals, but I only picked at my food. I am always nervous before big events. I settle down when the action starts, but until them I am like a cat with dogs around.

Dinner over, we sat down to discuss how our attack would be made. It was decided we would arrive early. Dragons are late sleepers, but we wanted to be sure to get there before she woke. Then too the cave entrance faces east. The morning sun should shine in helping us see well, while the dragon, looking out into the bright morning sun will have a harder time seeing us.

Once we got there Bravus on his destrier, Rienzi,would enter the cave on left side of the entrance. I would go in near the middle, and Herbeck would enter on the right.

"Is it wise for me to take the middle." I asked having second thoughts. "I don't have the strength or the weapons you two do."

"No," Bravus said. "It is the middle for you. You take that filthy cockatrice of yours and get it to cast its spell so the dragon can't fly. I am not sure she will understand what has happened, but she'll know something is wrong. It'll get Gwyrdd's attention. Then when she approaches to investigate, let her see you momentarily then duck behind one of those big boulders Herbeck saw just inside the entrance. When she comes for you, we will attack her from either side. It will be our best chance.

"Okay," I slapped the table top. "It actually sounds like a good plan. I'll wear my breastplate, and helmet, and carry my sword and shield. They will offer some protection. Plus when she sees me decked out like that she will know I am there to do her harm. Hopefully she won't see you two till it's too late, and your lance and arrows will already have mortally wounded her."

I turned to the cage. "What do you think, cockatrice?" I asked.

"I think attacking a dragon is the dumbest thing I have ever heard of. You will all be dead withing minutes of waking her. Take my wise counsel, free me and abandon this foolishness. You will thank me in years to come. However, you all seem to be set on this folly. I will do my part and earn my freedom." It was quiet for a second then went on, "It is, of course, understood that I will be set free the instant I cast the spell."

"Not exactly." I told the creature.

"What? You seek to change the rules at the last minute?

"No, I will free you. But it will happen, not when the spell is cast, but when it actually goes into effect. That way we know that you will not leave out some crucial syllable, vitiating the spell. And, of course, you know I will have the weasels with me, should either your memory or your cooperation fail us."

* * *

Sunrise saw us up. Herbeck and I helped Bravus into his armor. Since a horse as big as his destrier makes a lot of noise on bare rock, we stripped blankets off the beds in the cottage and used them to muffle horse's hooves. Then once Bravus was mounted we started for the lair. Herbeck and I went on foot. The fewer there were of us, man and beast, the better our chance of getting close without detection.

We split up as planned when we got there. Bravus and Herbeck each entered the cave on their appointed side and sought cover amongst the huge boulders to be found on the cave floor. Once they were in, I waited about a minute for them to get settled and then went in myself.

The air in the cave was cool and damp, reeking of the sulfur and death. The smell was so awful I had to breathe through my mouth to keep from retching.

The inside of the lair was huge. The cave's ceiling rose at least two hundred feet, disappearing into darkness above. The walls all around were steep and fairly smooth. At the far end I could just make out another cave branching off this one. Its entrance was about a hundred fifty feet up off the main cave's floor.

I moved carefully, from boulder to boulder. I wanted to be a ways in when I got the cockatrice to cast the spell. I also wanted to see the sleeping dragon so I'd know how and from where she would have to approach once we woke her.

Before long I was deeper into the cave than I had planned on going but couldn't see Gwyrdd anywhere. Dragons normally sleep late. Oh there are always exceptions, but a normal routine would be an afternoon of hunting and mayhem, followed by and evening of feasting off that day's catch, and then a late night of having it scales polished or teeth sharpened by the slaves it kept. They went to sleep late and slept late.

So then, Gwyrdd should have been visible somewhere sleeping, but she wasn't. Worried and looking around I noticed that a number of stairs had been cut into the rock wall of the cave, leading from the floor I was on and switchbacking their way up to that second higher cave. *Of course*, I thought. *She would sleep up there where she was safer. The stairs were for the slaves like my poor granddaughter to come and go, serving her.*

When I realized the situation, I must confess to the uttering of a few foul words that would upset my wife and our village priest, should they hear them. Would Angwyn's Vacuous Privation be effective enough to thin the air in such a huge area? I worried it wouldn't. We needed all the help we could get against the dragon. The cave was huge inside and she could just fly over us and rain down fire. Bravus and I would be helpless against such, and Herbeck's arrows might not alone be enough.

Well, I thought, *we must save Clairissa. The spell is our best chance. Let's find out if it's going to work?*

I set the cage containing the cockatrice down and took off the cover I had over it. "Well, it is time for you to cast the spell. Do so now," I told the creature.

"And you promise to free me?" it asked.

"Yes. And I promise to turn a weasel loose in your cage if either you don't do the incantation or don't do it right."

"Okay," the cockatrice said. "Just one thing, where is the dragon. I plan to flee in the opposite direction."

"I am not sure. I think she is in that other cave you can see up there." I pointed.

"You mean you don't know? That instead of running from her, I could be running right down her throat?"

"Go that way," I pointed again. "I came that way and can tell you for sure she is not there."

"Very well. I am anxious to leave. Many grave affairs have awaited my attention during the period of my confinement. I must see to them. So then…" and he began the enchantment in a strange sounding language. It took about thirty seconds for him to finish. When he did so I saw or heard nothing. Seconds ticked by. He'd failed.

I could feel a rage building in me. All that I and others had suffered because of the evil little creature was coming to a head. I reached for the weasel I had brought along in one of my pockets, but stopped. I could now hear a low rushing sound. Like a light breeze in a pine forest. Then the sound built. Now it was like a wind storm. Then came a howling sound from the entrance. The air was gusting from cave's mouth.

As the air thinned I felt a sharp pain in my ears. Suddenly I heard the dragon moving about, the sound of heavy breathing and scales rubbing against rock.

"Knavery," came an almost shout. The whole cave seemed to reverberate with the sound, yet I knew there was none. The dragon bellowed with his mind and I heard him with mine. "I declare a vexation," were the dragon's next words. "My ear drums feel as if they would burst from my head… Know that whoever is responsible for this outrage will pay."

As I heard those words, she appeared on the parapet of the second cave where it overlooked the main cave below.

Things would happen fast now. However, I am a man of my word. Before doing anything else I must free the cockatrice. I opened his cage. Carefully averting my eyes so as not to look into his, I told it, "You are free. Go now."

He needed no further encouragement, and was out the cage's door in an instant and running for the cave's mouth.

I thought to see some other movement in that direction, but had no time to worry about it. I must now attract Gwyrdd's attention, and get her to attack me and in doing so lay herself open to Bravus' lance and Herbeck's arrows.

I climbed the rock I had been hiding behind and stood where she could see me. I held my shield up and waved my sword menacingly at her. "I have come to kill you, you foul spawn of misery. Know that this day I will cut your fetid head from your polluted body. Before the hour is out, you will be turning on a spit in hell with a dozen demons basting you with your own juices."

"I think not," was her answer. "It is you who will taste fire. And no hour will elapse before you do. Prepare yourself. I smolder with rage. I am Gwyrdd of the Lancing Flames, Gwyrdd the Ash Maker. I come.

So saying she extended her wings and launched herself from the parapet. She gave one lazy flap and when nothing happen another and another increasingly desperate flaps of her huge wings. Her struggles were in vain. She dropped like a stone down to the cave's floor where she landed with a thud that shook the ground. She hit so hard that flames shot from her nostrils. I don't think that was supposed to happen. Dragons breathe fire from their mouths only. At any rate she cried out, "Foul man creature. What have you done?"

"Come to me," I yelled at her. "I am ready to hack your head from your body," and waved my sword at her.

Folding back her wings she scampered towards me. It was all I could do to stand on top of that rock while she approached. I so wanted to get down and run, but my love for my granddaughter and my will to help my friends sustained me.

As she got close I saw Bravus emerge from behind a huge boulder, I heard the thuds of his huge horses hoove's on the stone floor. Gwyrrd must have heard them too. Her head swiveled and she looked Bravus' way as he charged. Then before she could do anything about the knight there was a loud twang and an arrow zipped from Herbeck's bow and buried itself in her neck.

The dragon screamed in agony, but did not go down. Instead, in just a blink of the eye, she turned away from Bravus and towards Herbeck.

Another arrow zipped across the cave to sink into her shoulder. However, this time she only grunted with the impact.

Bravus was going fast now. With the weight of that huge horse behind it, the knight's lance would skewer the dragon like a cook getting a rabbit ready for the barbeque.

Suddenly though, as Bravus was getting close, Gwyrdd lashed out with her tail. A good foot in thickness and twenty feet long it struck, sending the horse, rider and lance tumbling across the cave floor. Bravus and the horse slammed into some boulders and lay still, either stunned or killed. I couldn't tell which. The lance ended up near me.

"Ha," roared the dragon. "He'll never mount that or any horse again."

A third arrow flew from Herbeck's bow. This one struck the center of one of her scales and bounced harmlessly away. The two arrows already in her might eventually prove fatal, but not immediately so. She had a lot of fight in her still.

Again Herbeck stepped from behind the boulder he was using as cover. He already had an arrow knocked and the bow drawn. It only took a moment for him to aim and again an arrow sang across space between him and the dragon. With a thud it sunk deep in her shoulder, just a few inches from the other she had already taken there. Not waiting to see her reaction, Herbeck ducked down behind the boulder again. Gwyrdd let out another roar of outrage and pain. Then I saw her chest begin to pump like a bellows. She took five deep breaths and then a sixth even deeper one which she held for a few seconds. Then fire poured from her mouth, a long column of it, flashing across the space between her and the boulder Herbeck hid behind. The dragon slayer was somewhat protected behind the rock. However his huge long bow stuck up and the flames burnt through its cord which I heard snap with a twanging sound. They also left the end of the bow burning like torch. No more arrows were going to fly today.

As soon as the flames ceased, Herbeck was up and charging the dragon. It would take her a few seconds to recharge and he must have intended to get at her with his sword before she could.

The dragon, however, turned her back to him and lashed out with her tail as she had at Bravus. Seeing what was coming, Herbeck raised his sword overhead and holding it in a two handed grip slashed down with all the power of those massive shoulders just as the tail caught him.

He went flying like Bravus before him And like Bravus also slammed into a boulder to lie still.

I was happy to see that the dragon had not gotten off lightly either. Herbeck's sword had cloven the tail through. The severed portion now lay on the floor, coiling and uncoiling in some sort of macabre reptilian death throes.

The pain must have been intense for the dragon made the keening sound as it turned to examine the wound. So far she had lost about five feet of tail, and taken three arrows. These wounds might eventfully prove fatal. The cave was anything but sanitary and the wounds could easily fester and lead to a miserable death. But they might not.

She had to die. Now it was up to me. I picked up Bravus lance. The thing was heavy. It must have weighed fifty pounds, and the steel tip did not make holding the end up easy.

I am old. I've seen over sixty summers come and go. I can still run, however. Or maybe I should say dash.   That might be a better word for it. I have strength, but not much endurance. I can go fast but not far. I do not think Gwyrdd saw or heard me coming. To wrapped up in pain, I would guess. But I did not want to try to sink the lance into her chest. I'd seen Bravus arrow bounce off those scales that covered it. As I drew close I yelled her name, "Gwyrdd, are you ready to die," I screamed. That got her attention and her huge head swiveled around to face me, her mouth open in what I assume was shock or surprise, Seeing that maul full of huge teeth and with fire glowing in its depths, I knew my target. As I said, I may not be able to go far but I can go fast. Before she could react I rammed the lance into her mouth, past her teeth and down her throat. Her hide may have been thick and hard to pierce, but the inside of her throat was not. The lance's steel tip slid over her hard palate then sunk deep in soft flesh at the back of her mouth.

Gwyrdd reared back. Her roar this time had a gurgling sound to it. She shook her head and the lance flew free. Then using one of her wings she swept me away like she had my partners. I remember flying through the air, I remember thinking Gwyrdd had won, I remember a vision of Clairissa and knowing I'd failed her and suddenly, in mid thought, I hit the ground and everything went blank or black or both.

* * *

I was sort of half awake, half asleep. I am not sure what woke me. Was it the thirst I felt. Was it Clairissa's beautiful feminine voice? Was it Herbeck's masculine voice? Was it the smell of food ready for the eating? Nothing made sense. I had failed to free her, so Clairissa was still the slave of Gwyrdd. Herbeck was dead, smashed against some rocks by the dragon. Maybe I was in heaven. If Clairissa was there, well then, it couldn't be the other place, could it. I drifted back to sleep.

* * *

I woke again. I was even more thirsty. But the voices were gone. I opened my eyes. Or should I say I opened my right eye. My left one was covered with something that kept it sealed. Still, I could see and looking around I realized I was in the expansible cottage. I was in the bed, in the room I used in the cottage. The door was open and I could see out into the main room. There sat Clairissa, in one of the easy chairs reading a book.

I tried to call her name, but only managed a dry croak. It got her attention, however. She dropped the book to the floor and jumped up and ran into my room.

Looking down at me she said, "Grandfather, grandfather, I was so worried these last five days that you would never come back to us." Then she started to cry.

I managed another dry croak.

"Oh, you must need some water. I'll fetch it."

"I'll get the water, you stay with your grandfather." It was Herbeck, standing in the doorway. His face and bare arms were covered in scabbed over scratches. One eye was blackened shut. Most of his hair was singed off. Most notable, however, was the sling that held is left arm.

When he left, Bravus stepped into the doorway to look at me. He was using a crutch to stand up. His leg was in a cast of tree branches tied with loops of rope. There was a large swelling on the side of his head too. However, lacking Herbeck's scratches, he looked the better of the two. Then Herbeck was back and Clairissa snatched the water from him, bustled by Bravus and back to my bed. "Here, drink this," She said holding a cup to my lips. I've drunk the finest wines, the smoothest ales. I have even tasted the fiery distillations of the Irish. I can tell you, nothing that's ever passed my lips tasted better than that water she brought me. My mouth was so dry, my throat so parched. It was just so cool and delicious.

When I'd finished the water, I found myself now hungry. I asked my granddaughter for some food. She went out and came back with a half chicken, some greens, and a flagon of ale.

My eyes lit up at the sight and my stomach growled at its smell. "You know me well, granddaughter," I told her.

"I can't take credit. It is the cottage. I walked out to get you some leftovers from our breakfast. Instead I found this on the counter. She then went and got extra pillows to prop me up. Once sitting and not laying in the bed, I wolfed down the food, feeling better with every bite. About half way through the chicken I stopped long enough to tell Clairissa, "Now that you've seen to my physical needs, tell me how I got here. How you got here. How Bravus and Herbeck got here. I am sure it is a tale I will want to here. My last memories are of defeat and knowing I had failed you.

"Finish your meal, and while you do I will bring chairs in here for the men. Then we may all sit and I will tell you everything.

* * *

When all were gathered round my bed she began her tale. "Right from the moment the dragon took me as I walked from my house to yours, I knew you would come for me. I was not sure when or how. But I knew you'd come. All the time I labored for the dragon… Polishing her scales was my job. Well, anyway, while I worked I kept a constant eye out for you. Days passed, ten of them, but I did not lose faith. Then, let's see you have been here, in this bed, out cold for five days, so it would have been six days ago I got this feeling that you were coming for me the next day. I don't know how I knew this. I just did.

So, I woke early that day and went down to the lower cave then out to look for you. Gwyrdd was awful to any of the girls that tried to escape. She would hunt them down or the forest creatures would catch them and bring them back to her for a reward. Nobody ever gets away, or so she said.

Still I was determined even if it meant the risk of capture and/or punishment. I felt this was the day you would come. I would find you. As I turned out, I was below you, down the hill when I saw the three of you entering the lair. I ran, trying to catch you, to stop you from entering. But I was too late. Then suddenly all the air was rushing from the cave mouth with a loud whooshing sound. Next I saw a cockatrice running out of gwyrdd's lair.

I've visited my cousin Angwyn's laboratory. He has a cockatrice. He taught me how dangerous they are and how you must avoid exchanging stares with one. He also showed me how to handle one, holding it upside down by the feet, and never looking into its eyes. *This could be a powerful weapon*, I thought. *It must not get away*. So, I chased it down and caught it.

Holding it as Angwyn taught me I returned to the cave. When the cockatrice saw where I was taking it, it set up and awful racket, protesting and saying it was just freed and this was an injustice, and had I no sense of the danger. It went on and on. I only got it to quiet down by threatening to dash its brains out on a rock.

By the time I got back inside you three's battle with the dragon was over. It couldn't have lasted much more than a few minutes. All three of you were down and out. Gwyrdd, was in a bad way too. But dragons have marvelous healing abilities. I feared that given time she would recover.

I also saw that she was determined to make sure you were dead, grandfather. I could tell the arrow wounds, pain of loosing a tail and whatever had her bleeding copiously from the mouth had left her hardly able to move. But move she was, and it was towards you. She would make sure you were dead, then probably do the same for Herbeck and Sir Bravus.

Seeing you lying there I knew you had come all the way from our village to save me. And furthermore, you are my grandfather. I love you. I could not leave you to the beast.

Holding the cockatrice upside down by its feet and behind my back I came around a boulder where the dragon could see me. "Oh, master," I told it. "What has happened to you? You are bleeding. How can I help?"

I was walking right towards her when she said, "Why should you help me? I enslaved you."

"But you are the most powerful creature in the world, how can I not worship you?" I asked her.

I was getting close now. "See how you alone have defeated three of these men. You are all powerful."

"Yes, well, of course," replied the dragon. Even evil creatures like her are susceptible to flattery.

"And, oh great Gwyrdd, you must eat to regain your strength. See what I have brought you to make you feel better," I said as I walked boldly up to her. When I was less than a yard from her, I pulled the cockatrice from behind me and held it up to her face.

I didn't know what her reaction would be. She might lash out at me. But I had to try.

The dragon looked to see what I had and her gaze locked with the cockatrice's. They stared into each other's eyes for a good ten seconds before Gwyrdd broke eye contact and retched on the ground. "That creature has the strangest eyes. I saw death in them. I suddenly feel much worse," she announced.

And she was. Uncle Angwyn told me the stare of a cockatrice can kill a person in less than a day. I found out it can kill a dragon much quicker. I guess it must have something to do with the fact they have a fire burning in their gut at all times.

Gwyrdd soon began to break out is pustules that rose from under her scales, causing them to fall off. Just a few at first, but they multiplied fast and soon they fell like rain and the ground was covered with them. She died in agony only a half hour after sharing stares with the cockatrice.

* * *

This story does not end with the dragon's death. I like stories where the good guys prevail over evil. Where the hero rides off into the sunset. Where they all live happily ever after. But this story has an even better ending.

I was in no condition to travel. Bravus had a hard time getting around with his broken leg and he couldn't ride anyway, his horse having been killed by Gwyrdd. Herbeck was not too bad off. Clairissa had set the bone for him and made a cast of willow and rope. So with two of us needing more time to heal, we must stay a while longer on the mountain side.

We moved the expansible cottage out of the cave it was in and into a forest glade. It was a nice peaceful place and I could sit on the porch and swap tales with Herbeck, and Bravus too, when he was around. Those times were infrequent, however. He spent much more time with Clairissa.

After two plus weeks of enslavement to a dragon, her clothes were in tatters, but she found some cloth in a closet off the room the cottage had made for her as soon as she joined its guests. Funny how it always seemed to anticipate our needs. So, with the scissors and other oddments of the tailor's art she had also found, she set about making herself some new clothes. She brought everything into my room and while she sat watching me and waiting for me to wake, she made herself a beautiful new outfit.

They were wasted on me, I was out cold. Herbeck did not seem to notice either. But Bravus did. He was not long in realizing that he was sharing the cottage with a woman much lovelier than anything to be found back at Melekhan's court. Then too, she was braver than any woman he had ever known. Her coolly capturing the cockatrice and then boldly walking up to Gwyrdd and using the little beast to finish off the dragon had taken nerves of iron. When he talked with her, he found her conversation witty and wise. No woman he had ever known had all these qualities and in such abundance. Is it any wonder he fell in love.

As for Clairissa, well she had always wanted a noble for a husband. Here was a knight that had seriously fallen for her. And she found him brave, handsome, and wise. Just the sort of man she had dreamed of.

When the alchemy works, it works. They were in love. They came to me to discuss it. "I know her hand is not yours to give away. That is up to her father. But I must ask you if you think he will agree to a marriage between Clairissa and I?" asked the knight.

"Yes," I told them. "Clairissa's father, Arwel, is a good man that only wants what is best for his children. That a noble would wed his daughter… Well, he will not oppose it. Oh, and as for a dowry fitting the wife of a noble knight, do not worry. I will see that she has a generous dowry.

Then Bravus grew serious. "Clairissa, please sit down. And you too, grandfather. Can I call you that?"

I smiled in answer. "Of course."

When we were both in chairs, he said. "There is something I have failed to tell you. Both of you. I deceived you. Not out of malice, but just not wanting to be paid any extra deference, or to be fawned over. You see, I am not Sir Bravus, knight of the court of Melekhan. I am Prince Bravus, son of King Broadrick, and someday, God willing, I will myself be king of Melekhan."

We were both stunned. Clairissa was to be not just wife of a noble, she would be a queen.

It was all too much for me to take and I called to Herbeck to fetch me a drink, and then another, and then a third. After that I don't remember.

* * *

The wedding you ask? Oh, it was one that will be remembered for all time. But that is another tale.

www.ingramcontent.com/pod-product-compliance
Lightning Source LLC
LaVergne TN
LVHW041210150826
845673LV00001B/342